"…ɑ   the painting ……, … …e ge… … …ha…e …he …ong. The song begins with *this* same picture, the same scene…a starry, starry night. And now we live it, with the heavens performing above us on our way to an island in the Mediterranean together. Happy and at peace. It doesn't seem fair."

"I'll take it. Fair or not, I'm glad I'm here on a boat with you talking about art, rather than living the turmoil that produces art."

"Turmoil didn't produce the painting or the song," she instructed. "A night such as this produced it."

Her words and thoughts touched me and reminded me why I left the happy life I led while on the kibbutz in Israel. Because I wanted this. What Michaela and I were sharing now—the peace of the ocean, the glory of the heavens, the sharing of our souls on a journey to some place new. Together. Adorned by God's own starry, starry night for our benefit.

Praise for Larry Farmer

Larry is a member of Texas Authors and the Brazos Valley Writers Club. He has four magazine articles published, two novellas, two short stories, and seven novels.

To Pam
From Larry

Starry Starry Night

by

Larry Farmer

larryfarmerwrites.com

1/15/2025

This is a work of fiction. Names, characters, places, and incidents are either the product of the author's imagination or are used fictitiously, and any resemblance to actual persons living or dead, business establishments, events, or locales, is entirely coincidental.

Starry Starry Night

Cover Art by *The Wild Rose Press, Inc.*

The Wild Rose Press, Inc.
PO Box 708
Adams Basin, NY 14410-0708
Visit us at www.thewildrosepress.com

Publishing History
First Edition, 2023
Trade Paperback ISBN 978-1-5092-4826-1
Digital ISBN 978-1-5092-4827-8

Published in the United States of America

Dedication

To Wolfgang

Chapter 1

I love the feeling of loneliness at times. Especially when shared with someone like Michaela. The Mediterranean soothed my melancholy as we watched Haifa fade into the distance. The beauty of biblical Mt. Carmel in the background made the loneliness all the more appealing, even romantic.

"You are lost in some memory, Nathan," Michaela said in a whisper. "Thinking of her?"

I attempted a smile. Michaela's long brown wavy hair was slightly wind-blown, which added an allure with her tanned skin.

"It was hard to say goodbye," I replied. "It was hard to say goodbye to everyone on the kibbutz. Even to Israel. But yes, it was especially hard to leave her."

"I know," she replied. "We made so many friends. We even lived history. It seems like Israel is always in some kind of history. And this time we were there for some of it."

I looked at her to share.

"Sadat landing in Jerusalem last year, you mean?" I inquired.

She nodded.

"That was when we first arrived, in the fall," she said. "That's how we met, remember? We watched on TV as he landed in Jerusalem. The year 1977 will be historic for that one event alone."

"It gave our stay some substance," I added. "Beyond being volunteers. We lived history right along with the Israelis."

"Then lived history again with every visit we made to a historical site—Acre, the Golan, Capernaum, Caesarea, Nazareth. Everywhere, it seemed. In this small sliver of a country, more history than in empires."

"We wanted a place to spend the winter before we traveled to Europe," I mused. "But when spring arrived, the orchards bloomed and the flower gardens exploded with new buds. It made me want to stay, instead. We should have waited until this summer to start traveling."

"Summer is too hot in Israel," she countered. "Spring is perfect for leaving." Michaela looked directly at me now. "Why did you leave her, Nathan? If we had waited until summer to leave, you would never have left her, I think. You were established already. If you are so in love with her, why are you leaving her? They even made you a candidate for membership on the kibbutz."

"I love the kibbutz," I answered. "It's been one of the greatest experiences of my life. I grew up on a farm back in Texas. I know how to drive a tractor, and the kibbutz needed me for that. But there is so much I want to do with my life. It's time to move on. You're right. If I stayed, I would get married and be there for the rest of my life."

"That's why kibbutzniks don't want their children to go with volunteers," Michaela mused. "Another broken heart to heal when the volunteer leaves."

"Is that why you didn't match up with anyone?" I asked her bluntly. "The guys there lined up to be with you."

"I adored them all. I am German. Jewish like them,

but so unlike them. I chose not to tempt fate. I could have fallen in love like you did. You have a heavy heart now as you leave, but you go home soon. She is alone on the kibbutz without you, and afraid to ever have a relationship with a volunteer again."

"That's what her parents want from her," I commented with a bite. "Stay away from volunteers and marry a fellow kibbutznik and raise children on the kibbutz."

"And that's why all the young singles on the kibbutz want to find a volunteer to mingle with. Flirt, but marry eventually with someone on the kibbutz. Have a good time, dream of life in some exotic place with a Prince Charming, or Princess Charming. But then you ruined everything, Nathan. You fell in love. You didn't have a fling—you fell head over heels. Then left. I didn't really like her. She was so offish to all the volunteers. She could have anyone. The guys drooled over her and she couldn't have cared less. We were intruders to her, I think. Then here you come. Tall, blond, an Ashkenazi Jew, athletic and muscular. Perfect. Even her parents had to accept you, since you were Jewish."

"She hated my blond hair," I replied. "And my blue eyes. Even my short hair. She had me grow it out after we got together. That part I could do. Grow my hair. Then cut it again when I left her. But blue eyes are blue eyes. I was stuck with them. She said blue eyes were empty. She told you to tell me that, in the beginning, in fact, and to tell me to quit flirting with her."

"That's because she is *Mizrahic*. Middle Eastern. She wanted one of her own. To protect herself. You are American. Jewish or not, you are so white. I suppose because of your white-skinned, blond-haired gentile of a father."

"Call him a *goy*," I instructed. "A gentile. A goy. I am Jewish because my mother is Jewish. I seldom go to a synagogue. I'm barely even religious, but because my mother is Jewish, I am Jewish. It's a race more than a religion. That's why Hitler wanted all of us killed. Not because of our religion, though that too. But because we are from an inferior race to the great Aryans. Ha. But here I am. Blond-haired and blue-eyed because of my father. Hitler would have had to kill my master race genes too. I thought those were supposed to be the recessive genes anyway. My mother's side included blond hair and blue eyes too, somewhere in the lineage through the centuries. And I guess God wanted people to know I am of mixed blood. A Jew by birth because of my mother, not a religious Jew, but racially so. And yet there's Aryan master race in the mix because of my goy of a father. So there, Hitler! This time you must kill a blond-haired Aryan to get at the—what did he call the Jews?"

"Vermin," she said with a giggle. "He called us everything in the book, but vermin was the most pointed. Yes, you did thicken the plot, Nathan. No one would ever guess you are a Jew by birth from looking at you. That's why Jews accept someone as a Jew if the mother is a Jew. Racially so, I mean. There is no doubt you are Jewish if your mother is Jewish. It is easy to assume your father is of the Aryan race, Nathan, by the blond hair and blue eyes in you, but no one can be certain of the father, really. Only the mother is a certainty. So if your mother is a Jew, then so are you. Religious or not. Rather clever to look at the mother to determine heritage."

"I stood out on the kibbutz," I said. "I may have been

accepted, as you say, and the kibbutzniks liked me and treated me well. But I stood out like a sore thumb."

"Her parents didn't seem to like you, but she fell in love with you anyway and then had to backtrack all the slanders she said about you at the beginning, like about your Nazi hair and empty blue eyes that she despised."

"And then I left her," I said, exposing my feeling of guilt. "After all that opening up she did toward me, I left her."

"*Scheisse,* Nathan. *Gottverdammt.* As soon as we get to Cyprus, I'm putting you on the next boat back to Haifa. You marry her, Nathan. Do you hear me? She loved you, and you are still in love with her. You grew up on a farm in Texas and will fit perfectly on the kibbutz. Just a bigger family to live with is all—a family called a kibbutz."

"I left our farm, Michaela. I loved it and my part of Texas, too, but I want to see the world, sow some wild oats. I may have loved life on the kibbutz, but I felt trapped. I was already feeling trapped just from falling in love with a girl there. That's a reason to leave. I felt trapped."

"I am starting to hate you, Nathan," Michaela said with a scowl. "I always liked you. And when I heard you were leaving, I decided to leave with you. We always had fun in the volunteers' clubhouse, you know, the *moadon.* The few times you visited, anyway. You are twice my size and were in the Marines. I felt safe thinking of traveling with you. But you left someone you love, Nathan. And someone who loves you back. You are shoving this in my face. You've left someone so in love with you."

I turned away from her emotional body blows.

Going back to the kibbutz was not an option. It—with the girl I loved—was now a memory. A warm, wonderful, haunting memory, but one to leave behind. I was hungry to experience new things. Things that provided adventure, not baggage.

"That's why you didn't go with anyone, isn't it, Michaela," I speculated. "You were the pick of the litter among the volunteers. You are a German Jew but look Israeli. Perfect height for a girl. Five feet four or whatever you are. Wavy hair, beige skin. It's like looking at some of the pictures of the first Jewish settlers in Israel. Pre-British Mandate settlers. Slim, hardy, gritty—so deliciously Jewish."

"But needing an American Marine to keep her safe. That's why I left with you. I'm sorry I did, now. I will never let myself have feelings for you. I am here with you for one reason only—you are safe. I like you but could never have feelings for you." She looked up at me. "I hope that pisses you off," she said with a laugh.

"No," I answered, shaking my head. "No, it doesn't. It makes me feel safe too. Now I don't have to leave someone else and mope about it again. You're helping me get past some of the moping right now. So we're the perfect match, Michaela. We adore each other and want to be left alone about it."

"Adore each other. Ha!" She looked up at me and smiled again. "I can live with that, I suppose. I know you didn't mean to hurt anyone. I can understand you not wanting to settle down. But you fell in love with someone, and it spoiled everything for you. I hate you for it, but yeah, I still adore you. And feel safe that romance with you will never happen to me." She looked at me pointedly. "And if you ever do fall for me, I will hurt you. Be warned."

Chapter 2

"I was disappointed there was no moon tonight," Michaela said from her sleeping bag next to mine. "But it is better this way. Aren't the stars brilliant? The kibbutz hid their glamour sometimes, but I loved walking there at night to see the stars. But even our little settlement there, as few lights as we had, diminished the full impact of heaven's glory."

"Yes, I love the view," I said, matching her sentiments. "It makes me glad we were too cheap to purchase a cabin room on the boat. We'll pretend we knew what we were doing. Back-to-nature freaks or something. And we don't even need the ocean right now. Just the stars, with no diminishing of the heavens from even the faintest lights. I used to sleep out in our yard on our farm sometimes, just for views like this. And sometimes there was so much work on the farm that we would have to drive the tractor at night. Lo and behold, there were the stars. Celebrating our company as if chaperones."

"Celebrating," she said with a sigh. "That is a perfect word for this. The heavens rejoice from our attention and devotion."

"I'm not trying to knock modern society. I'm glad we have prosperity in our lives. Schools, hospitals, museums, even factories to provide jobs and products we want. But I'm from rural Texas, and it wasn't long ago most of us were living out under these stars. The more industrial areas of America looked down on us for it. Like we were missing out on enlightenment."

"Do you know the painting by Van Gogh?" she asked as if off in her own thoughts. "*Starry Starry Night*. You know, like in the song 'Vincent.' As in Vincent Van Gogh, the artist. The guy that cut off his ear to get the attention of the woman he loved."

"If we ever fall in love, Michaela, don't hold your breath if you think I'm going to do something like that over you. And besides, I heard she wasn't his love object. She was his favorite prostitute. And he didn't cut off his entire ear. Just the lobe, which is bad enough. That just blows it for me, though. I wish I'd never heard the rest of the story sometimes. It ruins the image that was romanticized through the years—how he cut off his ear for the passion. But I love history too much not to hear the rest of the story. So I dig further, and the real story is never as good as the legend."

"He was schizophrenic, or so I've read," she contributed. "Actually, I heard it was some form of epilepsy from brain trauma at birth. It must have been horrible. Loneliness is bad enough no matter who you are. But to not even have a chance because you are mentally unbalanced? And through no fault of his own, while nothing could be done to fix it. We can pity him because he is so famous and so brilliant in his art. His legend and our pity just add to the allure of someone famous. But how horrible to be trapped in madness. No healing. Just expression. An outlet to diminish doom."

"And heartache," I added.

"Yes, and heartache," she said, as if identifying. "And so he creates his painting entitled *Starry Starry*

Night. We get to receive the beauty without the anguish he lived. Then the singer Don McLean writes a wonderful song about him as beautiful as the painting itself, and we get to share the song. The song begins with *this* same picture, the same scene…a starry, starry night. And now we live it, with the heavens performing above us on our way to an island in the Mediterranean together. Happy and at peace. It doesn't seem fair."

"I'll take it. Fair or not, I'm glad I'm here on a boat with you talking about art rather than living the turmoil that produces art."

"Turmoil didn't produce the painting or the song," she instructed. "A night such as this produced it."

Her words and thoughts touched me and reminded me why I left the happy life I led while on the kibbutz in Israel. Because I wanted this. What Michaela and I were sharing now—the peace of the ocean, the glory of the heavens, the sharing of our souls on a journey to some place new. Together. Adorned by God's own starry, starry night for our benefit.

Chapter 3

We landed at Larnaka, on the eastern coast of Cyprus, toward the middle. The location was made to order in that it was on the beach and on the way to the broader parts of the island of Cyprus.

"Cyprus is small," Michaela commented.

"Less than the size of Connecticut," I said. "So I read, anyway."

"That doesn't do me any good," she chided. "I suppose I have heard of Connecticut. But small is small. And it is small even for a European country. Large for the Mediterranean, though. It's the third largest island. Hopefully the hitchhiking is good. The British call hitchhiking 'autostop,' by the way. In case someone says that and you are dumbfounded."

"You can do the hitchhiking for us. You and your shorts and loose blouse."

"You make me feel like a prostitute."

"I hope I'm making you feel like a survivor. We aren't just tourists. We are two foreigners, young, and on a small budget. Backpackers. If I were alone, I would look like some goon. You will make people feel less threatened. And quite appealing to some deviants, also."

"I don't want a ride from a deviant, Nathan. Surviving or not. You also serve a purpose, you know. You are here to protect me if someone wants to check me out for more than a ride."

"Aw, she gets it," I said with a smile. "That's what survivors do. What gets you a ride and what you must put up with once you've got it. We have our own division of labor in this survival backpacker's world. Division of labor is a good economics term for you."

"Enough of this conversation. How long should we stay in Larnaka? On the beaches near here, in particular."

"We'll play it by ear. At least three days, I'd think. Unless there's danger or boredom."

"Boredom, he says. You are with me. Forget this obnoxious word."

We walked out of the port and on down the road toward the highway. This road would lead us to where we wanted to go, since we didn't care where we were going. Any sign that pointed to the city was to be avoided, however.

"Are you American?" a man from a car at the highway juncture asked as we approached.

"I am," I replied.

He seemed to ignore me as he looked at Michaela.

"I am from *Deutschland*," she answered him with a smile.

"Germany, you say. Where do you go now? Do you need a ride?"

"To a beach nearby," I answered.

"We are walking," Michaela added. "We enjoy the sun and the exercise. We just got off the boat."

"Which beach?" he asked while still looking at Michaela.

"We aren't sure," she replied. "We just came from Israel."

"Oh, Israel. Are you Jewish then?"

Neither Michaela nor I replied. Being a Jew could

be dangerous in this part of the world.

"I am going to Larnaka. Are you sure you do not want a lift?"

"Quite sure," she answered. "We want to spend the night on the beach."

"Oh, not on the beach. You need a warm bedroom. I have an empty room in my place."

"It is warm on the beach," she answered him. "And we love the ocean. We are looking forward to it."

"Get in," he insisted. "I'll take you."

"It is but a few meters," Michaela said pointedly. "We prefer to walk. Thank you."

"We're okay," I reinforced. "We just want to be alone on the beach."

"No trouble, matey," he said with a mischievous grin on his face.

"We are quite fine," Michaela insisted further.

His smile turned to a frown as he drove off.

"I'm glad you turned him down," she said to me as we continued our walk to the highway. "He was too friendly. Some people think backpackers mean free love and drugs. A good time. I'm sure some of the backpackers he has met here added to that opinion."

"The friendly, quote unquote, way you are dressed, Michaela, adds to the image they have of people like us."

"It's how I dress. I will add a bit of depth to his narrow view of the world. Or his view of our world. I am glad you are a Marine. Not just big, but a Marine. He can stereotype that image as well. More reason to prefer a beach. A more private beach, at that."

"How do you know all these words and phrases, Michaela?" I asked showing amazement. "English sounds like your mother tongue. Except for your accent."

She looked at me curiously.

"I live in Germany," she explained. "So many Americans there. Soldiers, but not just them. We are taught English in our schools growing up. We learn French as well. Plus, our television. We see so many Hollywood shows. How is one not to learn this language? And all its idioms. See, another word. I am majoring in English. I told you that in Israel."

"You said you were majoring in crafts. Or whatever it is you call it."

"Crafts is the closest word. That is my minor. I want to teach. Not just at home but abroad. I want to see the world. English opens the world to me. I don't want to be stiff in my speaking. I want to flow. English is the language passport to so much of the world. No matter what culture, English opens it up to so many people, thanks to the Americans. And, of course, the British, in the past, with their bloody empire where the sun never set."

"Where are we going while we're here in Cyprus, Michaela?" I asked to get back to our task at hand.

"To the beach first. We will talk there about where to go next and bring out again our travel guide. Or I should say *my* travel guide. You are so unprepared. You didn't seem to care at the kibbutz when we talked there either."

I shrugged.

"I just want to go," I replied. "To get out. Home is where I hang my hat."

"You don't have a hat, *monsieur*."

"But I have a thumb. I want to go."

"Okay, but when we find our beach, we are going to do more than bask in the sun. I want to see places on this island, and we will go through my travel guide to decide where we want to spend our time. I must be back in Freiburg by the fall to continue at the university. I took a sabbatical to Israel to learn more about my Jewish heritage. So I want to enjoy myself, but not just by sitting around. We will bask in the sun a bit while we are near the beach. We traveled around Israel, then took the boat here. So a bit of rest is in good order. But I want to see this island. It is a small island, but large enough we must be wise where to go. Turkey took over the northern part, a third of the island, just four years ago. We must have a visa for their portion, so the island for us is even smaller. But we will choose wisely. We have only a week to spend here. We must get to Athens on the mainland. I want to see the Acropolis."

"I want to see Sparta," I said.

"Who cares about Sparta? It is interesting history, I suppose, but there is nothing significant there."

"I just want to know I've been there."

"I wanted a Marine along. This modern-day version of Sparta. So this is the cost of doing so. Yes, I suppose Sparta will be interesting to visit. Maybe there is a museum."

"Hey, look ahead of us, Michaela," I said, pointing.

"There is the highway," she said gleefully.

"Left or right on it? Larnaka is not that big, but big enough. So to avoid the city, do we go right or left?"

"Let's go to the right. That's north. We're not so far from the Turkish area. Let's make it to the border there, then over to the center of the country. There are mountains in the middle of the island. Very pleasant. Rivers begin there, and forests cover many parts of those mountains. There is a waterfall in a wilderness park. We can camp out—beautiful spring weather with mountains, rivers, and lakes. There is energy on this island. Our island. The trees and meadows blossom with flowers. We can feel glorious to be young and eager. We will cherish these days, Nathan. They have cherries this time of year. I don't know what else, but cherries are ripe for harvest this time of year."

"So where is this place we're going, then? It sounds like you have it planned."

"Yes, of course I have it planned. We're going to Troodos. Not so much the town but to the wilderness near it, and the mountains there. Mt. Olympus is there, near there, but not the Mt. Olympus of the Greek gods. The tallest peak of the Troodos Mountains gets to almost two thousand meters."

"That's six thousand feet. Comparable to Denver in the Rockies. The mile-high city."

Cyprus as part of Europe didn't seem very prosperous. But a beach is a beach. Neither Michaela nor I had much money, so the price was right, too.

"I'll do the hitching," she told me boldly. "And you know why, as we discussed. Our division of labor, as you stated. We'll get rides, no problem. And if they decide on mischief, flex one of your muscles. We're a team."

Two cars passed us before we got a ride.

"I go to Famagusta," the driver of the car said in a strong accent. "Where you go?"

She turned to me as if checking me out.

"Hey, we're going to Famagusta next," she said. "Should we just take this ride now, since it's here?"

I shook my head no.

"I'm set on the beach," I replied. "You'll get us to Famagusta soon enough."

Her smile was broad. As if that's what she wanted to hear.

"Can you take us near a beach?" she asked the man.

"Get in," the driver instructed. "You girl sit next to me."

Michaela moaned as we got into the car. I managed to hold back my snicker. We focused intently out the car window for an area where we might camp.

"Here!" Michaela exclaimed to the driver after a few minutes. The highway swerved more directly toward the ocean. A perfect place to stay. "We want to get out here. We will walk to the ocean from the highway here."

I felt taken care of. I admired Michaela's travel instincts. She had been in similar command during our days traveling around Israel.

The sand was packed where we walked. The many cars that traveled here made a makeshift trail to the beach area which we now happily accessed.

"Is this private enough?" I asked as we looked around the deserted beach we had chosen. "There is absolutely nothing here. At all. How are we going to shower? To eat?"

"How did you do all of that in the jungle when you were a Marine?"

"We had c-rats. And sometimes it monsooned."

"I'm not eating any kind of rats. We'll find something to eat. And we have an ocean to wash ourselves."

She was too cute to correct.

The springtime sun on the beach was overbearing, and there was no refuge. We needed some shade. But after walking half an hour, there was nothing to come to our rescue. We were stuck with the sun bearing down

17

upon us from above. The heat reflecting from the white sand below us was even worse.

"Look," Michaela said, pointing ahead of us. "Maybe a kilometer from here. A lighthouse."

I saw it vaguely and let myself be hopeful. But could we use it? Our pace increased with new energy.

"Hey, Nathan," Michaela yelped as we approached. "It is abandoned, I think. No activity that I can see. And it is not so tall. Maybe two stories high. No one around at all unless someone is inside it."

We increased our pace as we approached the lighthouse.

"Look, it has a vacant room at its base," she said with a gleam. "A house for us. We can camp inside."

"It looks old, Michaela. We need to check it out and get a better look. There is nothing at all around. Even across the highway there are only farms. No houses anywhere, that I can see. That means no food or fresh water."

"We have a canteen. There is still some fresh water in it. Enough to keep us alive for a day, I think. Nothing to wash with. We'll get sticky from the ocean. But come on, we're pioneers. We're roughing it. We'll do good with this. Something to tell our grandchildren."

Our grandchildren, I mused. That had a nice ring to it. That couldn't be what she meant, I decided. Not literally. And why did I like the thought of her and me having grandchildren together, I wondered. Was I losing my independence?

The closer we got to the lighthouse, the more it looked abandoned. What paint it had was chipped and dry. The lighthouse structure was dingy, as if weathered.

"A place to unload our rucksacks," she said in

celebration. "I am traveling light, but it will be nice to dump things and be free to wade in the water without worry of someone swiping them. It is so wonderful to have a place for shelter from the wind and sun."

There was no door at the entrance of the lighthouse. Only rusted hinges where a door had been. Just inside the door was a spiraling metal stairway, which led to the upper room that contained the light placement.

"Be careful," Michaela warned, as she led the way up. "The stairs, or even the railing, may be unstable. But the view should be wonderful."

The staircase wobbled with each step we took.

"Why would they just leave a lighthouse to decay?" I asked as we climbed. "It seems dangerous. People through the years would check it out like we are. Someday this will break, with no one around to rescue whoever falls."

"I wonder if this is an off-limits site," she mused. "But there were no signs to warn us. Even in Greek letters. Nothing at all anywhere to say anything. And across the highway only farm fields. Why no fence to keep us out?"

"We have no food, Michaela," I reminded her.

"That is a problem," she concurred. "And I saw no village around. Not even a farmhouse. I don't want to waste time and energy walking the highway looking for a store or farmhouse. There is hardly any traffic. I hope a car takes pity on us when we are ready to leave."

"I'm hungry just thinking about having no food. I can't believe we didn't buy anything."

"We had no idea we would be in such a desolate place." She looked at me and smiled. "But that is good, Nathan. Pretend you are in a jungle. A Marine against the elements. Surely they trained you for such times as this."

I shook my head.

"They prepared us for jungles. Not for deserted beaches in the middle of nowhere."

"Ha," she scoffed. "We are survivors. We will beat the odds."

The upstairs ledge acted as a circular balcony for the light room at the top. It was too narrow for our sleeping bags to be side by side, so we laid them out at a slight angle. This would keep our heads from being next to each other, though mine would be at her shoulders, which would make talking to one another possible.

We stared out while holding onto the metal railing of the balcony. The ocean waves were gentle and inviting us to indulge. The sand was pristine. After a moment, Michaela looked at me.

"I am ready to wade, Nathan. Our own special and private beach."

The sand beckoned us to take off our shoes as we arrived at the edge of the ocean.

"It feels good between the toes," she said, as if needing to share. "Nice hot sand that is bearable with the ocean spray. I feel so alive!"

The water's edge was warm with the sand firmly beneath it. "The water will feel even better," I replied, grabbing her hand and taking her with me as I stepped farther into the ocean. When it reached our knees, an occasional wave would swoop up to the bottom of our blue-jean shorts. We stood for a moment to take in the beauty of it all, then walked parallel to the shore.

"I don't want to leave," Michaela said with a sigh.

"All the more reason I wish we had brought food

with us. We could stay here for days. We'll have to find something to keep us alive. Or at least limit the hunger."

Michaela turned toward the field across the highway.

"Let's check out what Mother Nature prepared for us," she said.

"You mean the local farmers?"

"Mother Nature's messenger," she corrected.

"I grew up on a farm, Michaela. There was always someone raiding our fields to get a few ears of corn, or some tomatoes, or a few heads of cabbage. We'll find something somewhere soon. I'm sure we're not as stranded as we think. I don't want to rob a farmer's field."

The walk along the strand was relaxing and peaceful, a nice distraction from our hunger.

"We can barely see the lighthouse anymore," Michaela said. "We should go back. It will be dark soon, and we need to set up so we don't have to stumble around. Besides, I want to watch from the balcony as the sun goes down. It will be a good and sentimental moment."

"Not a store anywhere this whole time," I added.

"I'm okay. But I'm a girl. Are you all right?"

"For discipline's sake, I've gone three days at a time without eating," I replied.

"Are you still up to such a trial?"

"I'll manage. I like the thought of enduring, anyway. We'll worry about food tomorrow."

"I like this, Nathan. We are good partners. My father told stories of the Holocaust in Germany. Not death camps, but the daily living after *Kristallnacht*. You know, when official Nazi policy declared Jews to be

21

subhuman. And things got worse during the war. Daily deprivations, I mean. It was hard being a German during much of the war anyway, but especially for the Jews in the concentration camps. My father managed to stay out of any concentration camp, but I feel a bond now with him, just thinking about going without a meal. How did he survive even when he wasn't in a camp?"

"Someday I hope you can tell me some of his stories, Michaela. I don't want to intrude, but since you brought it up, I want to hear."

She looked at me with a half-smile.

"Someday," she assured. "Someday I will want to share."

The sky glowed while the sun set beyond the sea as we made our way back to the lighthouse. Once we arrived, we clung to the last morsel of sunlight from the upper balcony where we made our home.

"It's the Sabbath now that the sun is down," Michaela commented as we stared out into the darkness. "We were not a religious family, but we celebrated some of the Jewish holidays. My mother was Christian anyway. We didn't celebrate Christian holidays either, really, but we noticed both sets of holidays. My father would tell us about some of the Jewish rituals. After the sunset on a Friday, or on a Jewish religious holiday, as the sky darkened, we would wait until three stars were visible in the night sky. There are three stars out now, Nathan, so it is officially the Sabbath. It's funny how we never celebrated Sabbath at the kibbutz. Even knowing it wasn't a religious kibbutz, it is sad we didn't do more. We were aware that it was Shabbat there, but it only meant we didn't have to work for a day. But it is Shabbat now, and we are sharing it, and I want to acknowledge it, to be aware of more than that we don't have to work. To be at peace is the key, I suppose. I am so sentimental now, for some reason."

"We acknowledged the Sabbath in our home," I commented. "My father wasn't a religious Christian, so he wanted to make my mother happy. She wasn't religious either. So I had two unreligious parents, each showing respect and appreciation for the sake of the other. Sounds odd, but a good sign of respect. We celebrated Christmas and such and gave token acknowledgment to Jewish holidays when my mother mentioned them. Being American, my mother loved Christmas as if she were a Christian herself. A tree and presents, you know. Carols. Easter we would watch something on television. Just to feel part of the community."

"Many Jews are like this," Michaela responded. "Even in Israel, the American and European Jews celebrated Christmas and Easter. Not in a noticeable way, but with a wreath or a song now and then."

I nodded my head at the memory.

"My mother let us know if it was Yom Kippur or Purim or some other Jewish holiday," I related. "Otherwise, we wouldn't have known. Now and then she told the story behind the holiday. I am grateful for the stories she told. They gave me some connection, at least, with who I am—or who I'm supposed to be. I guess that's why I chose to come to Israel when I did. Being Jewish is more about an ethnicity than about religion. You can be religious too, and many are. I identify with being a Jew. My parents didn't raise me to be either Jewish or Christian. Society drew a line, and I stepped over that line by choosing to be a Jew, which I am by birth because my mother is, though not religiously so. I want to understand that past better. It's my path, connecting more with the other me. The real me. The racially Jewish me. I identify even more now as a Jew culturally since I've been to Israel. I'm not just a Jew from some genealogy. I feel the part culturally and historically. So I'm glad you and I are both Jewish even if not religious. There is no such thing as being a half Jew. You either identify as a Jew or hide that you are even connected. I don't want to hide my Jewishness. It seems too all-or-nothing to do that. And I like sharing this with you. The nationhood part, the cultural angle. There's more to being a Jew than religion, and I'm glad, because I'm not religious and I like being part of the people and the history. Especially after Hitler."

Michaela nodded her head in understanding.

"Yes," she said. "But in my case, my father was Jewish. He survived the Holocaust, and I'm still not considered a Jew by some Jews because he, not my mother, is Jewish. I had to convert to pass all the tests. I'm not religious, but I converted just so I could honor my father by being a Jew with him. After all Hitler did in Germany during the time of my father, it was my determination to do this. To most Jews, I wasn't a Jew since my mother was Christian. So I spent a year converting so that my Jewishness is official. Let there be no doubt to anyone, in other words. It was my statement. To honor my father and his horrific childhood. The Nazis wanted him dead for no other reason than his Jewishness. He wasn't religious, but to Nazis I am a Jew and worthy of death for my ancestry. But though I wasn't a Jew to many fellow Jews, I could be dead now, since the Nazis almost ruled the world once. Is this crazy? Because of all that, by culture, by genetics, and by the rules of the game, however you want to look at it, I am fully a Jew now. Though I appreciate the religion, I am still not religious. It is the people that make me want to be a Jew. The ethics and pride. The history. To be a member of the tribe."

I reached over to hold her hand. She greatly touched me with her story. Michaela was indeed a very special person.

"So even though it is the Sabbath, we don't have to pray or anything, Nathan. I just enjoy the peace now, knowing the day it is. Religion is too stiff. But the religion is the glue to being a Jew, for sure. If I wanted to be a black person, I would still have white skin. Or in my case, light brown skin. I could relate to an aspect of black culture, or run around with black people, but I would still be white, not black. I could get off to the music or culture, even move to a black neighborhood, or similarly, I could be Chinese if I chose. But I wouldn't be that either, even if they accepted me. But a person of any race can suddenly be a Jew simply by converting to Judaism, the religion. No matter what your race or upbringing, suddenly the whole history and stigma is thrust upon you. You are fully Jewish from then on. So I appreciate the religious aspect of being a Jew for that alone. It is special enough to know peace because of Shabbat even if you are not religious. I appreciate elements of the religion and culture. I can take or leave the religion. But I love to be fully a Jewish person for the culture and history—the family of it all."

We fell silent as we listened to the ocean waves in the darkness. There was no trace of the moon yet, and we could see nothing as we looked outward. But we could hear the waves break upon the shore.

"Do you want to go wade?" I asked. "Our first night here?"

"We already did this. It is dark now. We could make it up and down the stairs well enough, but I feel settled already and just want to prepare for bed."

She felt her way to her sleeping bag and crawled in.

"Come," she said. "I am lonely. I want you next to me."

We lay down without touching. We could sense one another.

"The stars are so brilliant above," Michaela said as we lay next to each other.

"There's nothing around but us."

"The ocean accompanies us. It makes a soft noise like a lullaby. I love the peace and stillness of the night. I love the stars here, Nathan. Like on the boat. So few clouds. Just the stars, the ocean, and us. It's perfect."

"I'm glad you asked me to come with you, Michaela. I would have enjoyed myself doing this alone, but it's better with someone. I would have gone straight to Greece, I think. I don't know. I may have flown, even. Or if I was going to fly anyway, then perhaps straight to London or Paris. But this is wonderful. I knew there were Greek islands. Maybe I heard of Cyprus somewhere. Oh, for sure, because of the war here with Turkey a few years ago. But I didn't think much about it. I probably wouldn't have cared. The Mediterranean has an appeal, but Europe is the big goal. What made you think to come to Cyprus, anyway?"

"I wanted to work as a bargirl in Athens. I still do. I had a friend do that. A friend from my university. In northern Europe we love the southern countries like Spain, and the Greek islands. The sun. Oh yes, we worship the sun. I am so sick of the cold in Germany and the long winters and clouds. What keeps us alive is knowing we can go south to the Mediterranean countries. To Athens and maybe some Greek islands along the way. And sure enough! Look at us now, in Cyprus. The first stop. Now I can tell my own stories."

"So are you going to work as a bargirl in Athens when we get there?"

"Would you mind?" she asked.

"I would be in the way," I answered her. "You'd work late, then sleep most of the day. Guys will try to pick you up."

"Would that be okay with you?"

"Why wouldn't it? We're not attached. I could visit the sites and enjoy myself. But how long would you want to be a bargirl? You said you had to get back to your university. And I don't want to just hang around Athens waiting for you. There's something called the Magic Bus in Athens."

"Yes, of course. The Magic Bus. Three days nonstop through Greece, Yugoslavia, Austria, Germany, and finally to Amsterdam. But you are stuck on the bus the whole time. Three horrific days of eating, sleeping, and putting up with other penniless backpackers. You use the toilet on the bus, too. No girl toilet and boy toilet. One toilet for one desperate passenger at a time. If they stink the toilet up, too bad."

"But it's cheap," I emphasized.

"It's only about a hundred dollars, I think, however much that is in Greek drachma, their currency. So."

"Well, if we fly—if I fly, then I won't see anything of Europe except London or Paris. And I am a poor wayfaring backpacker. So Magic Bus it is for me. And it sounds like alone."

"I am sorry, Nathan. But I really want to see Athens. It excites me to think of working in a bar there before I go back to the university. I can't stay long because of getting back to school, but I want at least some time to be there, perhaps a week, and then fly home, to save time."

"Yeah," I said with a sigh. "I would want all that too."

"Let's see if I get a job in Athens first."

"I won't even be able to see the stars in the sky if I take this Magic Bus," I complained.

"You wouldn't from an airplane either, *mein schatz*. Or from another bus. You would have stops along the way, but you would stop in towns to sleep. The city lights and bustle of the cars would not be so romantic. Not like things are for us now."

"What is 'mine shots'?" I asked.

I heard her laugh.

"My poor American. Stranded in Europe and out of his range with our diverse languages. '*Mein*' is German for 'my.' '*Schatz*' is left over from old German. It used to mean like a treasure and such. So it is now used as a term of endearment."

"Really!" I yelped. "You just used a term of endearment on little old me? This long tall Texan in your midst?"

"Oh, yes, my lovely Nathan. I am quite affectionate to you now. You have been the perfect companion. I love sharing things with you, and I love our talks. And our starry, starry nights—like a Van Gogh, but real with you. You are my protector, one I never have to fear concerning any hormonal urges that surely you would be obsessed with…you know, being alone all the time with such a goddess as me."

I gave the necessary chuckle at her mock humility.

"I don't have hormonal urges toward you, Michaela," I said firmly, hoping I meant it.

"So, Nathan, are you implying I am not desirable? How dare you?"

I laughed loudly, to celebrate the topic as much as enjoy the humor.

"Well, Michaela, my dear, I do have to admit, you're rather hot. If I hadn't been in the Marines for so long and stuck having to deal with a macho man's wilderness while being one, maybe you'd have more to worry about. I learned to behave myself so I wouldn't leap on the first woman I saw every time I was back in civilization. Some Marines didn't behave themselves, and it disgusted me. Not only that, some women back home didn't like military men, in my day. We fit the goon factor with a lot of the jet-set females back home. So I adjusted by controlling my hormones."

There was silence for a moment.

"I am sorry to hear this, Nathan. Not about your controlled hormones, but I heard stories about the goon aspect of soldiers while growing up, so I did not care very much for the American soldiers in Germany. Many of them did seem like goons, and not as good about controlling their hormones as you are. So that is another reason I am glad we met and are now traveling alone together. You have broadened my horizons about the American soldier."

"I'm not a soldier, Michaela. I'm a Marine."

"Is there a difference?"

"You've already noticed some differences."

There was more silence.

"Nathan," she said softly. "I don't want to encourage your hormones. It has been such a symmetry between us so far. I want to keep it this way, this safe way between us. The friendship we share. But let me kiss you. On the cheek. Not to tease you, but to display the affection I do feel for you. And to say I am sorry for how you were treated as a Marine."

"Okay," I replied, "but only on the cheek. Or my hormones may win out after all. Right here with the stars watching us."

I heard the rustle of her sleeping bag. I felt the soft touch of her hand on my chest, then her moist and tender lips on my cheek.

Hormones, I instructed myself desperately, *don't fail me. Let me survive.*

Chapter 4

"Did you sleep well?" Michaela asked me as we sat up from our sleeping bags that acted as mattresses. "Even on the balcony it seemed stuffy most of the night. Maybe we should consider sleeping on the beach tonight."

"That means we're staying another night," I mused aloud.

"*Bestimmt*," she said forthrightly. "I mean, of course, Nathan. I thought we already decided to stay for a couple of days. I love it here. We still have to find food for ourselves, though. And maybe a more comfortable arrangement for our sleep. But this is our home."

"Well, that sounds cozy as hell," I chirped. "Sign me up then. Our first home together as a couple."

"As a couple?" She snickered. "Ha. Is that your hormones waking up? So now we are a couple, are we? Must I worry about my virginity?"

"Virginity. Okay, hmm. I won't slander you, but I don't think your virginity has anything to worry about."

"I could use a better word, for sure. So now. New subject. I am hungry. We will consider where to camp out tonight, but I still like this lighthouse. For the shelter and even the elevation."

"We can leave our backpacks up here while we walk around then," I replied. "But we walked a mile or so past this spot yesterday and saw nothing. No lodging, no restaurants. Not even a farmhouse to beg from."

"But we haven't inspected the fields, Nathan. We must do so first thing. Right across the highway from us. It is not maize in these fields or meadows. It is some sort of vegetable, I think. The leafy plants above the ground are not edible. At least not for us. Maybe for cattle. But I am thinking it is a root crop that is planted. I am a city girl, so I don't know these things. Anyway, let us check it out. I want to enjoy myself while I am here and not worry about starving to death. Hopefully the farmer's field across the way can keep us alive for a day or more."

We made our way down the lighthouse stairs and walked to the open field across the highway from us. I studied the leafy plants we were among, then bent over to pick one up.

"Potatoes," Michaela exclaimed excitedly. "How wonderful! They are high in carbohydrates for energy, but the skin of the potato has plant protein and vitamins as well. We can live here for days, Nathan."

"How are we going to cook them, though?" I whined. "We have no fire."

We scoped out the surroundings further.

"*Scheisse*, Nathan. Only ocean, beaches, and potato fields." She looked at me with a smirk. "Well, my boy, we are truly back to nature. I hope you like raw potatoes. I hope I do."

"I had survival training in the Marines. I never had raw potatoes, but survival is survival. It kind of brings back good memories. Survival is fun."

She let go a laugh.

"I surely came with the right person. Yes, my Nathan, we will survive. And have fun doing it. I will complain some if you allow, but this will be fun."

We bent down as if we were peasants and began

pulling up potatoes from the field and dropping them into our shirts that we stretched outwardly from our bodies to use like a basket.

"Six potatoes each," I said while looking at her. "That's enough for now. We still have to eat them raw. That won't agree with us so well. Our digestive systems, I mean. Let's take them back to our camp and look for something else to go with them."

"First we must wash them while we can. In the ocean. A little salt from the water will add some taste for us."

I thought back to our days on the kibbutz. There was spirit in her then, and I had been drawn to her because of it. I loved seeing it now.

"While we're out and about," I noted, "shouldn't we look for some other type of food?"

"I don't want to carry these around while we look, Nathan. We may have much to carry should we find something worthwhile besides these potatoes."

"Okay. The lighthouse is just across the road from us. We can leave our potatoes inside the doorway. There's no one to steal them. And they aren't worth stealing anyway."

We walked back to the lighthouse and entered the doorway.

"We can lay the potatoes next to the door," I suggested.

"They soiled my T-shirt," she complained while wiping off the dirt from them.

"We should try one while we're here," I suggested. "I'm hungry anyway, but we need to check out how we're going to handle raw potatoes. How we're going to digest them. Are we going to get indigestion?"

"Aagh," she replied. "Potatoes are potatoes. They will be harder to digest, but we have to eat anyway."

She exuded a grimace as she bit into her potato, but then broke into a giggle.

"They are horrible," she said. "Not really. I can handle it. So take one, my Marine companion. Before we look for lizard tails or whatever is available to lighthouse cavemen like us—cavepersons, I suppose, since I am a woman."

She then bit defiantly into the potato again.

"Ha," she bellowed with a scoff. "I can do this."

"A tad bitter," I said with a smirk as I bit into mine. "I can handle it. Juicy."

I took another bite, as did she.

"There," she said with a sigh after a few more bites. "That's enough. Let's find something else. Some meat, I hope. I have no idea where there is meat for us. I'm sure there is no chicken walking around lost. Nothing is going to come out from their habitat and give themselves up to us. But let's look."

We walked back to the highway but stayed on the beach side of it to do our search. It all looked the same as before. Vast fields of potatoes.

"There is nothing, Nathan. Absolutely nothing. We could walk along this road forever, I think, and it would all be the same." She looked at me. "Mr. Jungle Survivor, where do we get animal protein from dirt and potatoes and barren road? Asking for a friend."

"Well, I hate to dampen your hopes, but we're going to have to reenter the potato patch and look for insects or something. That's all I can think of."

"I am not eating raw insects," Michaela said emphatically.

She looked at me, her disgust evident.

"Okay," I replied. "We can quit now, then, without looking further, or we can enter the potato patch and look for whatever. We don't have to eat anything, but we can look just to see if there is a pleasant surprise somewhere. Or at least not horribly unpleasant."

She jerked her head with a determined nod.

"Let's do it," she barked.

The sense of adventure minimized any dread I felt. I had no idea what was in a potato patch besides potatoes, but I was certain insects were all we would find as an alternative. Even Davy Crockett didn't have to put up with this, I was sure.

"*Merde,*" Michaela groaned as we walked deeper into the potato patch.

"Why *merde?*" I asked her. "Why not *scheisse* if you need to curse? Or just plain bull paddies or something. Why French now for your cursing?"

"Because I need new words. New horizons for my frustrations. Not even insects in this *Gott* forsaken potato patch. I didn't want to find insects, but I was hopeful for something I could cope with. But there is nothing but nothingness here."

"Aha, look here," I said chirpily as I bent over to the ground. "A snail."

"Where, Nathan?"

"See, under the leaf, here, of this potato plant."

"Yes. Yes, you are right. Yes, a snail. Not escargot from a forest, but a small snail to feast on these farm plants."

She looked at me, gleaming. It soon turned to a sneer, however.

"But we would have to eat it raw," she moaned.

"Hey, we'll worry about that back at the ranch."

"What ranch, Nathan?"

"Our lighthouse. Let's just gather what we see and maybe we'll figure something out."

Bestimmt," she replied. "We shall cross that bridge whenever. Let us gather up our protein feast."

But our hunting party bore little fruition.

"How many?" Michaela asked after several minutes. "How many of these damn snails?"

"Six," I answered. "Six snails. Each the size of a cherry."

"Let's go home. It is in the afternoon now. I still hope we find something in the lighthouse left over that can produce a fire to cook with. Let us save our remaining daylight for this. Finding a way to prepare a primitive meal."

"That's a word." I snickered. "Primitive."

"I am not even talking about the food, Nathan. I am talking about preparing the food. If I am going to eat raw potatoes, I want more than raw field snails with it."

Of all the debris in the lighthouse, nothing offered promise as fuel for a fire.

"Raw snails it is," Michaela said with a laugh while taking a deep breath to help her psyche up.

I grimaced and nodded acceptance of our fate.

"We should put the meat from the snails inside the potatoes," Michaela suggested. "First we snip off the guts portion. I have scissors we can use. Then dig out a hole in the potato and bury these slimy morsels inside. We can even cover the meat back up with the potato we scraped away. Then we won't see it. Maybe that will help our cause in surviving this."

"You're the one that should have been in the

Marines," I commented, showing my amusement at her suggestions.

"It is instinctive, Nathan. We are equipped to survive."

"Yes, but you have it down as second nature."

"I suppose from growing up after the war."

"What do you mean?"

"The whole country was on the verge of starving to death. It took charity from the conquering allies to keep us alive. I was born after the worst of it and too young to remember much. But survival became second nature. My parents and other parents had so many stories to tell. We were industrious and motivated. We did much to pull ourselves up, but the immediate years after the war were so deprived it took massive aid to keep us alive. I take nothing for granted now that we are prospering again."

"I love being with you, Michaela. Everyone thinks of America as rich. I know we are, but it is a big country. I grew up in the poorest area of it. I'm not complaining, and I don't have stories to tell like you do, though my parents had stories for me about their hardships. It is another reason I am doing all of this, you know, traveling on nothing. It challenges me. I want to be challenged. It builds character."

She stared at me as if scoping me out.

"You indeed have much character, Nathan. You are not like the others. I don't mean other Americans only. I hear stories of cowboys and of Marines and that perhaps answers part of the difference between you and so many of our generation. But it is beyond that. You are idealistic. You are educated and intelligent. Skilled. But yes, you like challenges. Here you are. I admire it."

Her compliments embarrassed me. I wanted to have

a humble answer, but my silence was deep and answered her best of all.

"What shall we do now, Nathan? With our afternoon. The sun is warm and soothing. I love our simple life, but we are almost out of water. To drink, I mean. I think tomorrow afternoon we should begin traveling again. I hate to cut our time short, but it would only be by a day or two. If we run out of drinking water, we will not enjoy ourselves, even if we think we love our challenges."

"My canteen is almost full," I replied.

"But it is a small canteen. I am surprised the Marines gave you such a small canteen."

"They gave us two of them. We had them on either side of a cartridge belt. For balance. I just brought one since we have water easily available."

"But not here, it seems. My canteen is almost empty. I don't mind leaving early. We will see a beach again. I am not for just sitting around anyway. I thought surely there would be a village or a stream nearby. Basking in the sun is not so endearing if we don't have drinking water. We may even be stuck here. I see so few cars drive by. If we can't get a lift easily, we may run out of water. How are we going to get to Famagusta?"

Michaela would get us a ride easily, I was certain.

Chapter 5

"It is sad to see what was once so wonderful a city," Michaela said in a melancholy tone. "Famagusta was once the most important port city on the island. The main port to the Levant, you know, where we just came from—the Israel and Lebanon area. And a major port for the Silk Road in the trade with Asia, all the way to China and India. It is tragic about the war here in Cyprus a few years ago. I want to know I saw this divided city. We can see the Turkish part of Cyprus from here. I am not sure where to go next, however."

"I wouldn't mind seeing something of the Turkish part of Cyprus just to know I did so. I don't know who back home would care. But I'm here, so I care."

"Yes, but it is depressing to be here. I want to know I saw something, and then leave."

"It is going to be hard to hitchhike out of here, though," I commented.

"Yes, Nathan, yes, it will be. I am almost glad. I am sick of the autostop. It got us into the city, but I don't know if we will ever get out that way. We should take a bus out. I am ready for a bus. But I want to see some of the history here first. Cyprus is in the Bible, and it was a part of the Crusades. Important to the British in their empire. A gateway to the Middle East. But it is depressing now."

"I don't know enough about the place to know what

I want to see."

"We must find the Gazimaguza District. That is what my guidebook says. I don't know so much of the history either. Just that the British still have some troops here from back when they controlled much of the island. If we find the old walled city, that is where the Turkish portion of Famagusta begins. It is designated by the Turks as the capital of their portion of Cyprus. The old Venetians had a stronghold here until the Ottoman Turks took it over. I believe all of the old city is Turkish now. The Greek portion may not be technically Famagusta."

"Where are we going to stay?" I asked her. "Is there a beach nearby?"

"I don't want to stay on the beach. We did that already. The beaches at or near the city may not be safe. We need a hostel."

"Let's just walk," I suggested. "If we can't go into Famagusta itself since it's Turkish, let's just go up to it and turn around and leave. Not much going for us, I know, but enough for two backpackers on the way to Amsterdam, I suppose. I mean I am interested, but I'm not here on a mission. Just backpacking it on a shoestring with you."

"I suppose, my dear, but I am a bit frustrated with all the history here. From the Crusades and the Ottomans to the British. Even Greek history. I would like to see something and let it make an imprint. But let's not endanger ourselves. We are just backpackers."

"You are lost perhaps," a voice from behind us said.

We turned to look. The accent sounded British. It was a pale-looking middle-aged man standing a few feet behind us.

"Not really," Michaela replied. "We just arrived by

autostop. We have no visa to enter Famagusta itself, since it is part of Turkey."

"Is that important?" the man asked.

"We're here, and it would be nice," I replied. "We aren't staying. We intend to go to Nicosia next. Probably not tonight, since we're stuck here. We don't know how to get out."

"That's easy," the man said with a laugh. "Go back the way you came."

"We hitchhiked. We don't know our way around."

"Well, let me show you, then. I am here on business. I know my way a bit. I'm from Bristol. By the English Channel. But I grew up in Cyprus."

"Thank you," Michaela answered.

"I am on foot myself or I would take you around," the man said. "But come. I can show you the Green Line area where the Turkish part begins."

"Wonderful!" Michaela swooned. "Just a look and a snapshot and we will be on our way. We have no ambition except to go to Athens."

A broad smile broke out onto the man's face.

"The young hip generation," he said with a chuckle. "Yes, how exciting to be young. Not a care in the world."

"Well," I said in reply, "we have enough cares for our situation right now."

"Of course. I can direct you. Let's find a coffee shop. Or perhaps get a pint of bitter?"

"A coffee would be marvelous," Michaela said.

"Yes, then, let us find a place near the Turkish frontier for you. There will be guards, in fact, to protect them against the likes of us. I hope you like my sarcasm."

"I would like to see such a guard," Michaela replied. "Will he allow a picture?"

"I am sure, but we will be discreet. Take your picture from near the coffeehouse. He won't know."

The man led us to the next block, then to a street perpendicular to it.

"So you are a Greek Cypriot?" I inquired as we walked.

"Yes, I am. There is a Turkish minority living in this Greek portion, which is most of the island. Wait, we are almost to the coffee shop. We will talk there. Just follow, please."

A tour guide of sorts, I thought. That was comforting.

"Here is a restaurant for coffee," the man said as he turned to speak to us. "I cannot stay long with you, as I have a business appointment for lunch. It is a pleasure to see tourists here, however. Young tourists traveling off the land. Is that a correct judgment of you? With your blue jeans and backpacks. How nice that the hippie crowd would take an interest in us."

I instinctively wanted to correct his categorization of us as hippies. I had short hair and that was one of the reasons why I did, so people would know I wasn't a hippie or even a mod. But most of our appearance did seem to portray that designation, I realized.

The man took us into a café and walked to an empty table. He waited to pull out the chair for Michaela.

"You are American, is that not so?" he asked after we were seated, while looking at me.

"Yes, I am."

"But I am German," Michaela corrected. "We are traveling together since Israel. We recently left by boat from Haifa."

"Oh, so that explains why you are here," he said.

"Passing through and seeing some things as you return home. That is a good thing to do. Not just pass through and take pictures. We need people to know about us."

He smiled once more in approval, then began again. "Cyprus is not a part of Greece, perhaps you know. It is not one of the many Greek islands."

"Yes, of course, we know this," Michaela replied. "But the Greek part of Cyprus is so Greek in culture. At least it appears so to those of us that do not live here."

"There is a definite influence of Greek culture here. Cyprus is a large island for the Mediterranean. I know it is small compared to America."

"I read that it's the third largest island in the Mediterranean," I said to him.

"Yes, it is. It lets us live a bit. The smaller Greek islands are at least a part of the broader country of Greece. A boat ride away. We have had many sovereign countries in charge of us here in our history, including a large influence by the British. A way station for troops and trade for their empire. There are still bases here for them. That is how I ended up living in Britain. With the British contacts I made here while growing up. But Cyprus is sovereign. And that was our problem in 1974 with the war between Greece and Turkey. We wanted more uniformity on the island here. America has a mixed population, Europe very much so. And it is similar here on Cyprus, a mostly Greek culture, with some Turkish, and even some Arab. Our Prime Minister overstepped with trying to make Greek culture dominant. We were warned by Turkey not to do this. Greece and Turkey are both members of NATO, the military alliance between the Western Europeans and America and Canada, as you know. We considered it would be worked out. But

Turkey invaded us instead. So as small as our island nation is, it is even smaller now with the sliver of land in the extreme north of our island as a part of Turkey. Physically a part of Turkey now. Not a sovereign alliance, but a state of the broader country. It pains us, and we hope for better. Our hope is still to reunite, but the people are so divided now. Two distinct cultures, Turks and Greek. So I am not optimistic."

"It is very sad," Michaela commented. "And yes, here we are, all a part of NATO. So sad to have all these alliances, yet see this island still divided from the misunderstanding. That is a poor word, is it not? These hostilities date back through millennia. I am very sad about all of this. Even more we want to see some of Cyprus while we are here. It is in the news sometimes, but hard to visualize, really."

The waitress brought us three small cups of coffee and set them in the center of the table.

"Please, let me pay," the man said while reaching for a coin purse inside his upper shirt pocket. "Just a sip or two, and then I must leave."

"And you know," Michaela commented as she picked up her cup to take a sip, "to an outsider like myself, I don't see much difference in Greek coffee and Turkish. Even the grinds floating at the top in both. Both coffees are so similar I am not sure which is which. And Greece seems to me to be more Asia Minor than truly European. Perhaps that is just German arrogance to decide this. Greece is such a popular place to vacation for us. Not just because it has a warm climate compared to ours, but because it is truly different. Even more different than Italy to northern Europe. The music seems more like Asian than European. Stuck out here in the

Mediterranean Sea, Cyprus definitely has an Asian influence."

"Yeah," I concurred. "This is the first Greek coffee I've had. Unless I had one in Israel and thought it was Turkish. To back up what Michaela is saying about similarities, I am sure y'all can tell the difference, but I don't see so much difference in Greek and Turkish coffee. With both the food and the music, Cyprus seems like another area of Asia to me. Just like she said."

"I understand what you mean," the man replied. "Cyprus is very south in Europe, but also far to the east. Some of the smaller Greek islands go all the way to Turkish waters. Between Greece's own empires past and the Ottoman more recently in Turkey, Greece does have an Asian flavor to it in comparison to the countries north of it. Greece seems to have been shut off from the rest of Europe."

"So then," Michaela said, "while we sip on our coffee, and before you rush off, can you tell us how to see the Turkish portion of Cyprus? Just so we can have a look. Just to know."

"Yes, this café where we are now is only a block away from the frontier. Go out the door and turn right. Keep walking, and you will see the barrier with a Turkish guard. You must not enter, but you can take a picture if you have a camera. I am sure even a young tourist has some sort of camera."

"We both do," Michaela responded. "So a picture, then on to Nicosia."

"To Nicosia, you say?" the man inquired. "Nothing to see here for a tourist perhaps. Yes, take your picture. There is a bus station not far from the barrier. Someone will show you."

The man took a hurried sip from his coffee, then got up to leave.

"Good luck, my friends. I am grateful that such as you want to see our island and learn more of our situation. Enjoy. I will be returning to England soon. I am glad to meet such as you. I am somewhat encouraged now."

Chapter 6

"Nicosia has a portion inside the Greek part of Cyprus," Michaela commented. "Maybe we can find a hostel when we get there. Cheap. We have money for a night in a cheap hostel and to not worry about anything for a while, Nathan. Except how to get out of the city tomorrow. And find Troodos."

"I'm ready for a night in a bed," I replied.

Michaela looked over at me from her travel guide.

"It says Nicosia has been divided between the Greek section and Turkish since 1964."

"Ten years before the war divided the island," I observed.

"So all this animosity is here between the Greek and the Turks, and since ancient times even on up to now. Here in Europe, we are all trying to unite. Not just to protect ourselves from the Russians, but to be one happy people and economically prosperous. But there's so much animosity here on this small island among two NATO allies."

"Real problems have to be worked out," I mused, "not just speeches made."

"But beyond the ongoing crisis," she continued with her thoughts from her reading, "prosperity does seem to be happening."

She looked at me for emphasis.

"It shows it can happen. It is happening in the

European Union and it can happen here. The faster Cyprus settles their cultural divides, the faster prosperity will happen. Then peace feeds on itself. I hope anyway."

Delving into the turmoils of Cyprus as it lived in its divide was like a day of study for us. Sleep that night settled us down. We woke up refreshed in all regards. We were ready for new territory to cover and new subjects to partake.

The meadows were green as we peered out the window of our bus. It continued our tranquil moods. Life, warmth, peace. A welcomed feeling.

"We must find the old city of Nicosia when we get off the bus," Michaela suggested as we entered the city limits. "It will have everything we need as far as accommodation is concerned. Let's unpack in our room, then look at the old town as if it was a museum. That's enough. I want to take advantage of having access to a television and watch some news while we are here also. Just to see if the world is still going to exist a bit longer."

"Most important, though, a nice warm shower," I commented.

The bus station was near the old city of Nicosia. There were expensive hotels around, but a youth hostel was in the old city itself, and affordable.

We felt we had earned our shower after we checked in. There was a problem with that aspect, however. The shower stalls were communal. The men and women went into the shower room with the clothes they wore and disrobed on the spot. It did not seem to faze anyone. I felt awkward, however. Not because I had never dealt with coed living before, but because Michaela and I were still territorial with our privacy between us. We still needed our boundaries.

"I'll go first," Michaela said to me as she gathered her towel and clean underwear from her backpack.

"I'll seek out the laundry room," I told her. "If they have one. If not, I'll start hand washing my dirty clothes."

I felt pangs of jealousy as I pictured her naked in the shower stall in mixed company with other naked creatures in our hostel. The jealousy increased as I took my shower later in such free-spirited mixed company. Everyone seemed so hip and new age. Just how cozy was Michaela in all this free-love type arrangement?

"I found the shower endeavor quite an adventure," Michaela said over a glass of wine at a restaurant we found near our hostel later that evening. "Didn't you?"

"Adventure is a word," I said while allowing a smirk on my face. "Some of them were showing off. Some of the couples in there. There was a guy and a girl scrubbing each other down by the time I got in the shower. I was next to them, too. Then they would kiss passionately, then scrub some more. I had to pretend I didn't notice since what I wanted to do was gawk."

"Oh, I openly noticed the couple I was with in the shower," she said with a giggle. "I pretended everything was normal. Just biological harmony. Birds do it, bees do it, let's do it, you know. Oh, it was fun. I have been in communal showers before. In Amsterdam especially. That's where we are going after all of this in the Mediterranean."

She looked at me as if something was on her mind.

"I'm not going to stay as a bargirl in Athens after all," she proclaimed. "I could only do that for a week. I prefer going on with you on the Magic Bus. Not to rush. We'll go whatever pace, and if I don't stay to work a week in Athens, we won't have to worry about rushing things when we arrive in Amsterdam. We can do things together in comfort. So. The Magic Bus to Amsterdam. And then a hostel there. Maybe by then we will shower together."

She stared at me as if daring me to smile.

"Good boy," she said with a chuckle. "You are still behaving."

I burst out laughing.

"Tell me, Nathan. I am curious. Was the sex good there at the kibbutz for you?"

"It was wonderful," I replied. "I didn't necessarily think I knew everything about sex, but I was comfortable with my experiences. But I learned a lot at the kibbutz, I have to say. And I was glad. Girls are pretty liberated back home with our generation, but what I experienced on the kibbutz was beyond liberation. Yet it almost seemed innocent. It was so natural. Like breathing."

"Well, another reason you shouldn't have left. But I am almost jealous just thinking about you still there instead of here with me now."

Michaela had a gleam in her eye. As if enjoying the conversation. Our relationship seemed to be entering a new stage.

Chapter 7

"Which waterfall are you looking for?" the driver of our ride asked us.

"I am not sure," Michaela answered. "I don't suppose it matters. It is near Troodos."

"There are many waterfalls near Troodos. You are near Troodos now. Many waterfalls. One is five kilometers from here." The man pointed at the road behind us as we got out of his van. "I am sure less than that. If you walk you can manage. Even with your rucksacks. It is good to be young for such times. Good luck."

The road to the waterfall was narrow and unpaved, the weather warm and dry.

"We have food and drink this time," Michaela remarked as we set foot for our destination. "It is late in the morning. Even if we walk slowly, and even if we rest along the way, we will easily get there in the early afternoon."

"There's supposed to be a turn-off near the falls," I reminded her. "What if we miss it?"

"Don't worry, my dear, we will be there soon."

Sweat began to drip from our chins as we walked. But it felt good. Our bodies were alive.

We ventured two of the kilometers and not one vehicle appeared. Why was this not a popular destination, I wondered? Somehow the locals did not care. Familiarity breeding contempt or something. And Cyprus still did not have many tourists visiting since the war.

"I don't want a ride now," Michaela said after yet another kilometer walk. "We will be at the turn-off soon. I am satisfied that we are true adventurers and not of the bourgeois. Do you remember this word, Nathan? Bourgeois. Our generation was so set against the lazy and empty-headed masses. The revolution we were surely set to have for equality and justice required hardiness. Bourgeois is such an obnoxious word. I feel good to use it now, however. I do feel a contempt toward the thought of settling down to a normal boring and robotic life. Let us grab what we can of any adventure, Nathan. We will walk to this garden of Eden spot by the waterfall and get back to nature. Even to God, I suppose."

"I'm game. It will make the food tastier."

"We don't need a long walk for the food to taste good. Fruit is sweet and has a fresh aroma. The bread we bought is fresh. Not warm out of the oven anymore, but still soft. The pastrami is dry, but not spoiled."

"I wouldn't want a restaurant now," I commented. "I guess because I can't have one. But I like the thought of sandwiches. I like pastrami. It has a flavor. Back home while growing up, if we ate a sandwich, it was baloney."

"It was what?" she asked.

"Bologna you would call it. From Bologna, Italy, you know. It's okay meat, but rather plain. Pastrami is even Jewish."

"Look, Nathan, just ahead. Just to the right of our turn-off. I can see it now. A clump of trees in front of a cliff. And I am sure there is a waterfall there. I am so

52

happy about the trees. It will give us some shade. If we want to sunbathe, we can do that. Then the trees will let us cool off even without a swim."

"All the better there is no interest in this place by the locals. We have it to ourselves."

Indeed, if there was a Garden of Eden, Michaela and I had stumbled upon it. The cliff before us was so high we could not see the landscape or the source of the water flow. It could be a lake above us, for all we knew, or a river. But the flow from the waterfall was steady and fast, and I guessed it to be ten yards or more wide where it emptied into the small pool in front of us.

"I can't wait, Nathan," Michaela blurted as she dumped her backpack and dropped it to the side. "I trust you," she said as she began to pull off her T-shirt. "I am going skinny-dipping. Please join me. This is the perfect spot for you to see me without clothing for the first time. We will remember this place even more."

She unbuttoned her cutoffs, unzipped, and pulled them down. Then her underwear. It excited me.

"Join me, Nathan," she beckoned once more as she walked to the edge of the pool.

I casually disrobed, trying not to show emotion.

"Be careful," she cautioned. "The edge is slippery from the spray of the falls."

Slowly she stepped into the pool while holding onto the boulder at the edge for support.

"Oh, the water is cold!" she yelped. "I love it. I am getting goose pimples from it. It awakens the pores. It is wonderful. I am standing on the bottom here. It deepens quickly. How deep does it go? You are tall. Help me find out how deep the pool is."

I stuck out my foot from the edge like a coward and

grimaced.

"My God," I howled, "it *is* cold! It's so damn cold."

"This isn't Texas, Nathan. The water must still be freshly melted snow. Be brave. It's wonderful. Join me. There are mountains all around. Many waterfalls from them. This one is ours. Enjoy with me."

I jumped in just beyond her to let the shock devour me and get it over with.

"Oh, God, help," I cried out. "Aagh. Oh, God!"

"You are fun. But join me, Nathan. Hold on to me. It makes me want you. Not just for your body warmth. My Jane needs a Tarzan now. Please. Hold me."

I gasped from the cold a few seconds longer, then waded over to her open arms. She hugged me tightly as we caressed one another. Emotions gushed.

"Michaela," I said with a quiver.

She placed her head on my chest while rubbing her hand softly on my neck.

"Michaela, I'm vulnerable for you. This is overwhelming me. You are overwhelming me, I mean. Emotionally. Take pity on me. I'm trying to behave myself."

"I want you overwhelmed by me, Nathan. That's exactly what I want from you. I am glad you are vulnerable. I am also for you. It is good. We will make it wonderful. To be vulnerable and at one another's mercy."

I was afraid to say more. This wasn't a tease. She was making a play for me. I wanted it. I didn't care how it ended. With pain and regret or with ecstasy, this is exactly what I wanted.

"Wait," she said as she broke away from me. "I have a bar of soap in my rucksack. Let me get it and we will wash each other. Like we saw others do in the hostel in Nicosia. That's what broke me, you know. I wanted you then, but I tried to stay strong. I want you now and will have you this time."

She grabbed hold of the edge to crawl out. Once fully on shore she turned back to look at me.

"Watch me, Nathan. Look at me. See? Here I am. Yours. I want you to desire me."

Her body was light tan where it had not been exposed to the sun. A natural tan color. Not from sunbathing. Her more exposed areas were darker, more brown than tan.

She sat on the edge of the water with her feet dangling in the pool, then pushed out with her arms to splash into the water.

"Soap me down first," she instructed as she walked back to me. "Then I will do you. We are in paradise, my love. This is dangerous, Nathan, to fall in love like this. But that is what I have done about you, and I know you are in love with me. I have known it for days. Your feelings for me are beyond affection. You are in love with me, and I find that irresistible. Perhaps it is me wanting this from you, but never mind. You are in love with me, and if not, you soon will be."

She pulled at my neck to kiss me. I could not quit kissing her, each one more deeply than before.

"Yes, Michaela, I love you. I love you. I don't know what to do about it, but I love you."

"We know what to do, Nathan," she answered. "Yes, we do. We already know what we will do. Don't think about it or talk about it. Live it. This is so precious. It's as if we held back our feelings until we found this spot. But here we are—here we are and it's wonderful."

"I want to make love to you, Michaela, but I don't want to leave your embrace or this pool. We can't make love here. It's too unstable. I want to make love, but I want to stay here in the pool with you even more."

"Just live it for now. The wanting me. We'll make love soon enough."

She looked into my eyes, softly but firmly.

"And you will not leave me behind, Mr. Nathan man. I am here to stay in your life. We will go together, to wherever it is. I don't know the details yet, but I tell you this—you will not be leaving me, or I would not be doing this. The trusting I am doing about you. The letting go with you I am doing now. I am crazy to get involved with you knowing you just left behind someone you love. But I am not crazy at all. Because you will never leave me. You'll see. We have much to work out, I know. I am not as sure as my boasts. But I feel destiny between us, and this makes me bold. Believe what I tell you."

Chapter 8

"Here we are living off the land," Michaela celebrated, "and now that we have food again in our rucksacks, we don't notice the trees we are camping under."

"What about them? Like almond trees in Israel. But it's past almond season."

"Look at the trees behind these. Cherry trees. And the cherries are abundant and ripe. Perfect. So sweet and so rich in vitamins. Let's stock up."

We walked over to them. I pulled off several from limbs too high for Michaela to reach. She took them from me and washed them from the pool.

"Oh, man," I swooned. "They're wonderful. I don't know if we can get full on this, but it makes a great dessert."

"I already didn't want to leave this place," Michaela exuded between bites. "This is so much a paradise, Nathan."

"How much food do we have left from the store?" I asked. "How long can we stay, then?"

"We only have a couple of days' supply. It is so hard to decide how much to buy. We don't have room in our rucksacks, and it is burdensome, too. Plus, it spoils so quickly. So we must not buy much. But then we stumble onto paradise and have regrets we didn't buy more."

"At least we won't get bored. If we leave by

tomorrow…?"

"The next morning," she countered. "We will leave the next morning after all. Like we originally planned. We must spend another night here after this."

"Okay, another day to skinny-dip. Good. The full primordial paradise setting. And walk around fully clothed. Maybe not. Then skinny-dip to cool off again. No time for boredom. I'm glad we are in love. Something to do."

"Paradise was enough to keep away boredom. But yes, being in love is a perfect encore."

"So where's the best spot to camp?" I wondered aloud. "While we have our clothes on, let's find our spot so we can go au naturel again. Under the cherry trees or directly by the pool?"

"I love the sound of the rushing water from the falls. But we can also hear this from where the cherry trees are. They are not so far away. The trees will make us feel sheltered. Even like a fortress, perhaps, for our imagery while we sleep."

"But I want to see the stars," I added. "Another starry, starry night. Even a more glorious one. So maybe not directly under the trees. An enclave between some of them, where we can take in a hunk of sky."

"Such a romantic, Nathan. I don't picture this of a Marine. Or a Texan either. It is nice to see this in you yet again."

"I don't know a country boy alive back home that doesn't want the great wide open to sleep under. We have more stars in Texas than any place in the universe, I bet. And short winters to let us have this sky most of the year round."

"You make me want to see this," she said looking

directly at me. "I love hearing what makes you what you are. Your Texas that you describe explains a lot about you. I want more."

"We're living day by day, Michaela. Keep wanting. Somehow wanting is getting."

"Good. We don't have to make plans, then. We just have to keep being who we are."

"Oh, man, Michaela, I'm getting turned on listening to you and your seductive words. I wish it was night already."

"Let's make our camp, then. In this spirit. On the edge of the trees. With a big hunk, as you described, with a big hunk of sky alongside our delicious cherry trees."

We walked until the sound of the waterfall diminished, then turned around to walk back toward it, stopping where the sound was most appealing.

"Man, I never want to leave this place," I said as we sat on top of our sleeping bags at the site we chose.

"I am glad we don't stay long, though, Nathan. Somewhere in a long stay this would seem mundane. I want to remember this paradise at its best. Before we get used to it."

"Well, then, let's walk around while there's still some daylight left. Sweat it up, then skinny-dip again before camping for the night."

The sun was wonderful. It was hot, but bearable. The sweat made our skin alive and exuberant. With trees around us amidst the waterflow nearby, we felt a rapport with nature.

A last dip into the pool of water after our walk produced a pinnacle of bliss. We held hands as we swam underneath the water. I, at first, resisted the notion as too corny, but loved it all the more for being exactly that, once I touched Michaela's fingertips.

"We cannot leave this place," Michaela swooned as we cuddled on top of our sleeping bags that night. "No matter what I said about redundancy. Somehow the same stars we see tonight are glowing all the more brilliantly than even our first night, on the boat from Haifa."

With that I placed her hand onto my neck.

"I love it, Michaela. And I love being in love with you. It's perfect. It gives a fullness to everything. You would think the beauty of the place is enough, and the peacefulness, but being in love just makes it a totality. Was this all planned by some cosmos? It's too real. Too perfect. How can we top this off? I mean it surely can't get better than this. So what do we do next?"

"Don't spoil it, Nathan. Each day will be better in its own way, a new chapter for us to live while we're together. They will build on one another."

I jerked my head away from her at the thought.

"I don't want to be in love, Michaela. I was minding my own business, dreaming of worlds to conquer or die trying, and here I am totally happy. This ruins everything."

She sat up and pulled her hand away as she did so.

"What am I supposed to say to that, Nathan?"

I reached up to touch her shoulder, but she pulled back farther.

"I don't know, Michaela. This overwhelms me. I'm disoriented."

"You just left someone behind, and now I can't even enjoy my moment with you. I am so vulnerable, Nathan. We've always had a rapport and now it has blossomed. We've had these marvelous days together here in Cyprus. Why did you just spoil it?"

She got up to walk around.

"Please, Michaela. I'm sorry. Trite words after all this, but don't go. Please. Being in love disorients me. To feel this way. To be so happy. I don't know what to do with my life."

"I can tell you what you can do with your life, Nathan. But I don't feel like wasting my time doing so."

She grabbed her sleeping bag and pulled it behind her.

"Stop, Michaela. Wait. Don't go. I'm sorry. I love you. You know I do. It scares me to be in love."

"Shut up, Nathan! Shut up! Shut up!"

She threw down her sleeping bag and walked toward the pool of water. Since I knew that meant she wasn't leaving, I let her go her way, to work things through.

I wanted to beg her. It wasn't just pride that kept me from doing so. It was knowing that begging wouldn't work. It would allow her to punish me, but that would be only a shallow victory. We had to work this out.

How?

Michaela kept her stare focused outwardly over the pool of water as I approached her from behind.

"You're sorry?" she asked just above a whisper.

The sound of vulnerability in her voice encouraged me. She wanted to forgive me, I could tell. I answered her by pulling her hand to my lips to kiss. She then touched my cheek softly with that hand before returning it to her lap.

"It sounds so strange to hear my voice all of a sudden," she said.

"Being in love with you means everything to me, Michaela," I said to return our focus. "But it doesn't answer everything yet. I grew up in a world of transition, on that farm in Texas. And as a Marine going to a war no one but me believed in. I worked a year in Houston behind a desk, and it was the most miserable year of my adult life. So I went back to college to finish my degree, and then I traveled. And loved being challenged by the world and educated by that world as well. It was wonderful. But what next? If I hadn't been so miserable in Houston, maybe I would be ready to settle down. As it is, I am horrified at the thought."

"But we have to settle down someday," she replied.

"I have heard as much. And it makes sense. I don't want to be a bum, and I doubt I can be an adventurer much longer. But I still don't know what to do with myself."

She turned to look at me. Her sweet innocent profile melted me.

"And so what does that have to do with me, Nathan? I know you are in love with me. But I have a life too. I must go back now to finish my university degree. Then I want to find work in Africa somewhere. I am an adventurer also, just not a Marine Texan about it."

"How much more until you finish your degree?" I asked her.

"Another year. Some of it abroad. The English language is a part of my degree. By my design. I am majoring in Literature and chose the Victorian era as a dominant part of this. I need to study in an English-speaking country, with English as the primary language, I mean. Not a place like India or the Philippines where it is a dominant unifying language, but in a country where English is the official and primary language throughout the entire country. I thought about going to England, but I am also considering Australia." She looked at me directly now. "But I am thinking now of going to America for a semester. Because of you."

"I told you I'm going back to work on my graduate degree, didn't I?" I asked. "My master's degree?"

"You mentioned that you were considering it. But you wanted to go to Australia and through the whole continent of Africa, from Morocco on down to Cape Town. You have talked about many possibilities for you. With all your dreams of adventuring mixed in. So everything you told me is about how you don't know what to do with your life. As was pushed down my throat yet again a few minutes ago."

"So, Michaela, what if I go back and get my master's? And while you are finishing your degree, when it is time for you to go to this English-speaking country, then maybe you can study with me in Texas."

"That sounds wonderful to me, Nathan. Precious thoughts for me. So see, here we are in love and making plans too, and not permanent ones. There was room for being in love after all, and still we can dream our dreams of what may be in our lives, without knowing all the answers yet."

"So why was I such a jerk?" I asked her with a giggle.

"*Genau so*," she replied. "Exactly that. We could live together in Texas, then. That would give us a long rope about making or not making more permanent plans. Do you like my little Texas expression? We could use a long rope, get it?"

"And do you know the rest of that saying about the rope?" I asked. "A rope used to hang ourselves. Give a man enough rope and he'll hang himself."

"Precisely, Mr. Cowboy. We'll see who gets hung

then."

"So I'll stay with you until your school starts and then go back and apply for grad school back in Texas. And play it all by ear. Is that a go? My God, we're making plans, Michaela. I love plans after all. And perfect ones. Happy ones that don't include permanency."

"Live this day to day, Nathan. Trust our feelings. Let them have their say. Fears about settling down will still be there. But we have time. Time to sort through it all. Trust our fate, then."

Chapter 9

"This is the highway we want," Michaela informed me as we walked to the adjoining road at the crossroads. "Do you remember it? This is where we started walking to the waterfalls two days ago. We continue on now to where we would have gone, to Limassol. We are quite a ways from there right now. Unless we get good rides this afternoon, we will be stranded somewhere. There are no major towns, even for Cyprus standards, along the way. We had better buy provisions at the first chance."

"Well, you are a bit sweaty still from the walk we had before our ride. I don't know if that will help us or hinder."

"You are still depending upon me for our success, then? It was you who wanted to walk just now."

"I was afraid we would never get a ride," I replied. "I knew the road was short enough to walk if we had to. We already walked it."

"Well, companion, that is why I am sweaty. I hope our ride wants a nature girl."

Before we extended our arms to appeal to the approaching car, it slowed down as if to stop for us. A man in a priestly robe yelled to us through the open window. I had no idea what he said, but Michaela replied to him, then looked at me.

"He is going halfway to Limassol. This road we are on is not the road to there, but he will take us to the highway that is. He is with a Greek Orthodox church in a town perhaps an hour away. This is good. We don't need my sex appeal, for once."

We placed our backpacks in the back seat of the car, with Michaela crawling in next to them. I was left to entertain our priest, even though he seemed not to speak any English. Michaela, to be polite perhaps, began talking to him from her seat in the back as he drove.

"I speak Yiddish," Michaela explained to me. "I was speaking Yiddish just now with the priest. For your information, his Yiddish is not so good. I mentioned to him how we were in Israel even a week ago. Since I don't know Greek or any Slavic languages, I hoped he might know German. He knows a bit, but surprisingly knows some Yiddish since he has lived in Jerusalem and spoken with European Jews there. Yiddish has many European words in it. He doesn't know English or Hebrew, so I don't know how he communicates while there except with Yiddish. It has some German in it and some Hebrew. Even some Slavic. We can communicate."

She turned her attention again to the priest. The conversation with him was short, and she turned quickly back to me.

"So, okay, Nathan. He is going most of the way to Limassol. He invited us to stay on the church grounds. That is very nice of him. There is a small town there. But if we are most of the way to Limassol when we arrive to his town, then let us keep hitchhiking. Or even take a bus to Limassol. We must buy provisions while at his town. I don't really want to stay at a church. He is a nice man, so that is not the problem. I even have a bit of curiosity about the church here, but not so much. Now that we just left paradise, I am eager to travel on. Perhaps we can make Limassol by tonight and catch a boat to Athens tomorrow."

"That sounds good to me. I'm so glad you're multilingual. You have sex appeal and linguistic skills. I'm just your goon."

"Well, my friend, do not apologize. I am very happy to have such a goon for me."

"Okay, I'm worth my keep, then. It all worked out."

The town where we were dropped off wasn't very big, but a store was all we needed. We bought bottled water, canned goods, cheese, bread, and beef jerky.

"Turn it on, Michaela," I said encouragingly as we once again solicited rides on the road.

"Someone," she said joyfully. "We have a ride. In no time at all we are back on our way."

"I go only a few kilometers," the woman said with a slight accent. "Would you rather stay in this town? You may be stranded where I take you. There is not so much traffic, and it is getting late in the afternoon."

"We want to catch a boat to Athens," Michaela returned. "We just go to Limassol. Anything to help get us there will help. We don't mind to be stranded. We just bought provisions. It's okay. Thanks for the ride."

Her car was just big enough to hold us and our gear.

"I have a farm," she told us along the way. "My husband and I. We raise chickens, mostly, but also a few dairy cattle. We also grow sunflowers. We have a few trees for lumber. Land is expensive in Cyprus. We make good money, but it is so expensive to live, and the taxes are so much. But it is a good life. We enjoy it."

We traveled for half an hour before reaching her farm. The short distance was time consuming because of the narrow highway being constantly immersed with farm equipment.

"Good luck on your journey," the lady said as she dropped us off on the side of the road opposite her farmhouse. "There is still daylight. You can make it to Limassol, with luck."

"Cheers," Michaela replied as we pulled out our backpacks. "Thank you so much. We will walk a bit to find a tree or something, since it is so hot."

"I do not believe there are any trees in this part. On the highway, I mean."

"We will try," Michaela returned.

We watched the lady drive to her house.

"I just wanted to be private," Michaela informed me as we walked. "I didn't want her to worry about us, in case we get stuck here. She has done enough for us. We have provisions. I would rather take care of myself."

The few vehicles that traveled on our road were local only. Or so said some of the drivers that bothered to stop to apologize for not picking us up. Some offered us a place to stay, but we preferred to keep on our way.

"I can't believe it seems so hopeless," Michaela complained after an hour of no luck.

"Not even curious men wanting to come to your rescue," I complained with her.

"Let's find a place to camp. I'm getting hungry. We can start fresh in the morning. And just like she said, this farm lady, there are no trees to shelter us. We must find a field. Probably our friend owns these fields."

Just ahead lay a patch of sunflowers. That would give us shade and keep us out of view from the traffic.

"There is no room to snuggle," Michaela complained as we lay on our sleeping bags in the field. "It is like they haphazardly threw out the seeds for these sunflowers. We barely have space to maneuver inside the field. The ground is hard with clods, and no room to snuggle. A worthy struggle after our night of paradise at the waterfall. To remind that we are knights of the road, I think. What do you think, my dear?"

"I think I love you anyway. So there."

"You are horrible. I need comfort, but you make me want to be next to you even more."

"I do miss snuggling with you, Michaela, but I'm enjoying this sunflower jungle. Part of the adventure."

"I am already your best adventure."

"Yes, you are. Even now."

"That's it. You said the right thing. So good night. Dream of me. And we will gaze at the starry night again. A bit of a challenge with our sunflower canopy, I know."

We felt the sun's heat the next morning even as the sunflower plants protected us from direct sunlight. I heard shuffling nearby, where Michaela lay.

"Are you awake, Nathan? Do you need more time? I hope to make it to Limassol today, and we may still be stranded. So let's be on our way. I'll break out the food. Cheese and bread."

"Yeah, I'm ready," I answered as I sat up to get my bearings.

"You know what we don't have," Michaela said with a whine. "Coffee. I assumed we couldn't brew and we already were carrying so many provisions, but I really want a coffee before we go on the road. I will be cranky, I'm afraid. Beware."

"Well, great. I wasn't thinking about coffee until you mentioned it. So I'm going to be cranky too. Great way to start."

"I don't want my breakfast without coffee. So I'll

Larry Farmer

tear off a portion of bread and beef jerky to have at the ready. Maybe we can nibble a bit along the way. If we get very hungry. But we must find a town soon."

We walked out of the sunflower patch onto the barren road. We nibbled on some of the jerky as we waited for traffic, more for something to do than to appease our hunger.

"Hallo!" a woman's voice called out to us. "Hallo there, my friends."

We looked toward the farmhouse and saw the lady who had given us the ride the previous day. She waved at us as she walked.

"Please, welcome," she beckoned further. "Please, come. Come to my home for some breakfast for you. I will prepare for you sausage and eggs."

"She said sausage," I commented as we walked toward her. "Do you suppose pork?"

"Are you so kosher?"

"No, but I wasn't sure you weren't."

"Nathan, you know me better. I love Judaism, but only the history and ethics. Not so much the strict diet. I told you that already. If kosher was for health reasons, then perhaps. But as I understand it from studying, the early Hebrew were a desert and mountain people. Pigs were not part of their cuisine. So the more they intermingled with their neighbors, their diet helped define them. I am influenced by this diet, but far too modern and jet set to stick myself to it."

"Sounds good to me. Sausage it is, indeed."

The lady smiled as we approached her.

"I am sad you did not get a ride," she said as we walked to her house. "I did not see you in the evening when I looked out. I was willing to invite you to spend the night. But suddenly just now, I looked out of my window and there you were. Ready to make autostop. I can prepare for you eggs and sausage. I must brew a pot of coffee. My husband is already in the fields since early this morning, and we drank together all that I prepared."

"Oh, you are wonderful to us," Michaela swooned.

"It is my pleasure. We are not blessed with visitors to our beleaguered island so often. That is a word, no? Beleaguered. I know such a word from a novel and on the television. Come, we are here. Let me open the door to let you in."

Michaela and I looked at each other, showing how moved we felt by the lady's kindness. Soon we could smell the coffee brewing.

"Here is a cup for each of you," she offered us where we sat. "I will just be a few minutes. Let me go to the kitchen. Would you like the radio?"

"Oh, no, ma'am," I said. "We're fine. It is relaxing to just sit in a nice house once again."

"That is a pleasure for me to hear this. Thank you. I will return quickly."

Michaela's focus was on an old dark brown wooden dresser across from us against a wall. Its top held a couple of vases on a white lace cloth.

"This is so old Europe," she said. "I love this, Nathan. What wonderful luck we have so far. As if we are on a guided tour, like some cosmic hand showing us the best of Cyprus."

She looked at me affectionately to share her passion.

"I am happy, Nathan. About everything. About Israel, about the boat ride, about the beach, and the waterfall, and now a feel for old Cyprus."

I nodded with a smile of approval for all she said and

mentally added my own memories to hers.

"Here," the lady said as she poured from a pot. "Do you need sugar or cream?"

"Thank you," we said to her in unison.

She soon presented link sausages, and we each grabbed one from the serving dish.

"Oh, it is wonderful," Michaela said loudly enough for the lady to hear. "It is so marvelous. I will remember this fondly."

"Man, this is as good as anything we have in Texas," I swooned.

"Thank you," the lady replied as she brought the condiments. "What joy for me."

"I hate to leave Cyprus after all of this," Michaela said to me just above a whisper. "But I do have to get back to my studies, and I want to see Athens a bit before we take our journey on to Amsterdam. I won't be a bargirl now. We are running out of time. Between the boat ride and our week on Cyprus, I will not have time. It was a nice thought. I have to get back to my apartment before school starts."

"What a send-off Cyprus has been!" I sighed. "How melancholy we were to leave our beautiful home in Israel. But now we experience all of this. God has plans, doesn't He? I know I sound corny and superstitious, but how do I not feel this way?"

"Yes, also me," Michaela replied. "I am a modern woman, but I am not soulless. It is for us to find our way. And skepticism is as good a vehicle as faith. Two sides on the road to truth. We make our way on this road, Nathan. Together."

Chapter 10

We stood side by side at the front of the boat along with many other passengers. Piraeus lay ahead. The excitement only grew as the port to Athens became more vivid.

"We must walk a bit after we debark," Michaela instructed. "Before we find a hostel. I don't know how far I want to carry our rucksacks, but we must look for a cheap hostel, and I am sure there won't be any near the port."

"But this is Athens," I mused, "the seat of government—the economic hub, too. And one of the world's most attractive tourist sites with all the ancient ruins. There must be all kinds of places for visitors. We're on foot, and we don't know what we're doing. Let's don't walk too long. Unless the accommodations are outrageous."

"Agreed," she returned. "We will walk until we see something that looks affordable to us. We'll ask along the way. If who we ask doesn't speak English, I will give it a shot in French or German. I don't know Greek, and I heard the Greeks are not good about other languages. But since this is a tourist and financial hub, surely some will know one of our languages. We can ask at a luxury hotel. They will speak other languages."

"After we find a place, before we go sightseeing, we have to find out about the Magic Bus, where we can get tickets and where to go to catch it."

"Yes, Nathan, you are right. Our logistics, you are saying. We must take care of business before we become obnoxious tourists."

It was hot, and sweat poured from us as we trudged along with our backpacks. Even though Athens was on the ocean, the buildings around kept away any comforting sea breezes.

Michaela looked at me as we walked.

"Nathan, we are going uphill. It makes sense, since we came from the port, and the incline is not so great, but with our rucksacks I am wanting a place to stay soon. There is a youth hostel here, I'm sure. They are very good about being in tourist areas and still well priced even if we are not members. Let us find one. We can see if there is cheaper accommodation tomorrow. But if the price is reasonable, I want to keep it. We have a long, horrible journey ahead of us soon on this Magic Bus. We will be stuck on it for three days. Three days straight from Athens to Amsterdam. It will be torture. Let us find a good comfortable hostel, and soon."

I nodded approval as we walked on.

"There," I said, pointing straight ahead of us. "The sign. That's one of those hostels you mentioned. The chain. The international chain or whatever. I stayed in one in Jerusalem once. We can't stay together, though, unless we rent a room."

"No, cheap is the word, Nathan. We'll stay in a dorm. We will be sick of each other anyhow, after three horror days on the Magic Bus. Let us have some peace now."

"Oh, Michaela, I'm sure you're right. The Magic Bus will be drudgery, and the honeymoon stage between us will be tested. But no. I love you. Period. Through thick and thin. Don't talk so gruff even if it's true."

She reached over to hold my hand.

"You said the magic words, Nathan. I love you too. Through thick and thin."

I was geared to sleep alone in a dorm room with other guys, but I still didn't like it. Roughing it or not, I wanted to be with Michaela. I made my peace with circumstances the best I could as I put my belongings into my wall locker. They'd assigned one to each of us. The sights of Athens would cheer me back up, I was sure.

"Do you know where we're going?" I asked Michaela as we walked the streets nearby.

"A girl in my dorm room showed me on the map where to buy the tickets for the Magic Bus. On the map in my guidebook, I mean. It's quite a walk. I might have to ask someone."

"I'm glad you're in charge of all this," I said. "I hated map reading in the Marine Corps. If the world wasn't round and there wasn't mass transportation, I'm not sure I would make it anywhere I wanted to go."

"You are pathetic. But I like being in charge. So it works out."

Map or not, it still took asking directions. Most people had never heard of the Magic Bus.

"At last," she said as we stared at a sign on our side of the street. "This is the organization that handles these rides." She looked at me for emphasis. "Let me do the talking."

"If you insist."

The Magic Bus had a set price that was very reasonable, by far the cheapest around for what we wanted to do. But still I trusted her judgment on things better than my own.

"We heard it is three days' travel," she said to the young clerk behind the desk.

"I am glad the word is out about our company. We have four buses, and they travel back and forth regularly. We travel almost daily. It is a hard ride, requiring several drivers who sleep in the back of the bus along the way. Except for the one that is driving at the time."

"Once a day there is a rest stop, you said before. Besides the small stops to change drivers. That means not getting to relieve ourselves much."

"I suggest not drinking or eating very much."

"Yes, we will take this ticket of yours. When do you leave next?"

"Tomorrow morning at eight. If you miss this departure, the next one will be the next day at the same time."

"We will be here. Thank you."

"But that means we can't take in much of Athens," I whined. "You were going to be a bargirl here and now you aren't even staying long as a tourist. It's such a historic city."

"I love your spirit, Nathan. That's how you were in Israel and Cyprus. I like how you want to take in things and not just have a photo or two. But I must get back. I have my apartment in Freiburg and my courses to attend to. We have time for the Acropolis, but not much else. We will dream about another venture to Athens. I know we talked about staying here for a couple of days, but suddenly, with my tickets to home, I am anxious to go back."

Michaela pulled out travelers checks from her money pouch strapped around her waist. She signed several of them and handed them along with her passport to the clerk. She turned to me then. "He will need your passport."

I retrieved my passport from my pouch, also strapped around my waist, but just as I readied to pull out some travelers checks she stopped me.

"I paid for both of us," she informed. "You can pay me back along the way or in Amsterdam. Or in Texas. My down payment for your sponsoring me as a student. See how it all works out?"

Our trek remained on an incline as we finally came upon the famed Acropolis of Athens, where democracy began, as far as Western civilization was concerned.

"They were truly democratic in the beginning," I told her. "One man, one vote."

"Unless you were a slave. And one man meant literally one man. Women couldn't vote. I will try to be objective and pretend that it is possible that women were not informed and educated enough to be part of the process. I suspect, however, the ancient Greeks were too macho and proud to include women in any power structure. I am grateful that anything began here. Greece did take a great leap in science, politics, and philosophy. So we will dwell on the leap that occurred, even if it left out at least half of the adult population."

"It's exciting to finally see the Acropolis," I said as I stared at the relic before us. "I was always a Sparta man, but Greece and the world probably were better off with Athens being the main center."

"Even more so as the precursor to the great Rome."

"I hate Rome," I said with a bite.

"Perhaps Jews should. But imagine the conquering Romans with an empire that had no Greece to inspire it.

Without the academies it inherited. The science. The philosophers. Imagine our world now without all that. We Jews found our way anyway. That's what we do. That's what I'm proud of. And our way was better because there was an Athens."

Michaela was the perfect one to share everything. The emotional charge inside me felt erotic, in fact.

Chapter 11

I dreaded what lay ahead as Michaela and I boarded the old passenger bus that would take us to Amsterdam. It looked more like a school bus from when I was growing up than a passenger bus oriented toward a long trip. All this was part of the price, the cheapest imaginable, but a drudgery now that I was getting ready to do it.

They crammed passengers into every square inch of the narrow seats. Three days, nonstop, of this arrangement. If I had any money at all, I would curse that I was taking the trip this way. But there was adventure here, too. So I was glad I was a bum.

Adventure. That's what we were here for. And that's what I loved about it. Even if I hated it.

There were no armrests to separate or comfort the passengers. The padding in the seats was very thin, supported by springs. The one good thing about the cramming arrangement was how it glued Michaela to me. I was stuck with a rather overweight guy to my right, however, which made the squeeze on me all the worse.

Once we began traveling, it seemed worth it. Movement. A goal. A destination. New territory. New experiences to tell my grandkids someday.

Music played over loudspeakers for us to enjoy, the pop songs of the day. This being cheap, uncomfortable travel, only young backpackers were partaking, so the music was for us. The hip. The comedy craze Cheech and Chong also played. This got me past my discomfort.

The hinterland of Greece was very pretty. I was charmed by the many mountains that greeted us along the way. These mountains helped me understand their history. At the bottom of the European land mass and at the northern extreme of the Mediterranean Sea, these Greek mountains helped protect against northern invaders. If invading from the south, a navy was required. That is why Athens became a naval power. Mountains and a powerful navy all but insured their safety.

Overall, the peninsular part of Greece was not very large. Within hours we were in Yugoslavia. My first time in a Communist country. Communist, but pro-Western. The only such country in the world.

"Most of our trip will be going through these granite hills in Yugoslavia," Michaela informed. "They are special somehow in their structure and makeup. So says my travel guide anyway. But I don't understand geology. They are noted for their beauty."

"Where I'm from in Texas is so flat. I always loved mountains. Great they're part of the trip."

"By morning we will be in Austria. Speaking of mountains, I have never seen the Himalayas, but only they have a chance of being more beautiful than the Alps. I know the Himalayas are bigger, but I can't conceive they could be prettier. I will check it out someday. But right now, I am going to sleep. It will make the trip shorter, too, if I sleep for part of it."

"I wonder if we are going to use the restroom somewhere. I knew not to drink much water, but sometimes nature calls anyway."

"Yes, I second that, my friend. By morning there will be puddles in the aisle all along the bus if we do not stop. I am sure there is a plan for our excretions."

But there wasn't. We endured the entire night with only one stop for gas. By morning there was murmuring.

"We will fill up with gas in the next town," the bus driver yelled out to us. "We will change bus drivers then."

There was exuberant shouting on the bus with the word that a rest stop was imminent. The sun peered over a mountain peak from our right, but all I could think about was my screaming bladder.

"Did you sleep well, Nathan?"

I looked over at her. Her hair was in clumps and her eyes had no spark to them.

"I slept better with coyotes in the Mojave Desert during infantry training," I replied with a bite. "Since you ask."

"Was I a good pillow for you? I was afraid to move all night long. Your head was totally on top of mine."

"Was that your head?" I asked with a sneer. "I dreamed my head was lying on top of a can of hair spray."

"Hair spray? I don't use hair spray. Where did you get such a dream?"

"No idea. I still love you, but you are not as comfortable as I remember from back when we snuggled at the waterfall."

"That is for sure, if we are comparing, Mr. Nathan. No, you were the worst night's sleep just now that I ever had in my life. Thank God you don't snore."

"We go from voluptuous starry, starry nights to you turning into a pillow that was somehow a can of

81

hairspray."

"Perhaps our honeymoon is over, then. All good things come to an end, as they say."

"Test away, Cupid. This will be a good memory anyway, don't you think?"

"*Genau*, my dear. Of course it will."

The click of the loudspeaker came on.

"We will be stopping soon," the driver remarked. "I am sure you are needing toilet relief. There is a store we attend on these trips. Toilet facilities are available. Please be generous and buy some items. Thank you. If you do not know, we are still in Yugoslavia, but we are approaching the frontier with *Osterreich*, or in English you say Austria."

"Thank God," Michaela and I gasped aloud, in unison with the rest of the bus.

"Remember," Michaela said as she looked at me. "It is all right to buy a sandwich, perhaps. But unless we are starving, we should minimize how much we eat. Or drink, especially. These relief stops are few and far between."

"That's for sure," I concurred. "This is only our third stop so far on the whole trip. And one of those was just to relieve ourselves in a forest along the way because someone complained loudly enough."

"It is still worth the cheap price, Nathan. I am enjoying our fellow adventurers. Everyone seems to be a survivor. These are special days. The hardships are bearable and make good memories."

We arrived in Austria just before sundown. As beautiful as Greece and Yugoslavia had been, Austria was the country I most wanted to see. I fretted that darkness might well deny that euphoric longing.

Soon the sun lowered behind the snowcapped peaks in front of us to create an orange glow of mist-like wonder.

"Is that an Alp?" a guy with an American accent in front of us asked mockingly.

I nodded that it was.

"Where are you from?" I asked him.

"Michigan," he replied. "You sound American."

"Yes, Texas."

"Yippee-ki-yay, cowboy," he mocked.

I hoped the disdain showed on my face.

"What brings you here?" he asked.

"I was going to ask you that," I said.

"I wanted to see Athens. I have a brother in Germany. One of the military bases there. I thought I would make a tour of some hotspots while in Europe. Rome, Paris, Athens. I'm going back to Frankfurt now to fly back home after dropping by my brother's again. And you?"

"I just came from Israel. My friend and I are going to her home in Germany now."

He stared at Michaela with a curious look.

"Germany?"

Michaela looked at him blankly for a moment.

"Freiburg," she answered. "It's where I go to university."

"Where are you from originally?"

"Moerfelden. That's near Frankfurt."

"You're German?"

"Yes."

"I thought Germans were blonde and blue-eyed."

"Not really. Many are, but most have brown or black hair. I suppose half or more have brown eyes. I don't

83

really know. It's such a mixture."

"But your skin is brown."

"We've been sleeping on the beach."

"But so brown."

"It is a lighter brown without the sun."

"Germans are white."

"I am Jewish. Many Jews, I suppose even most, are white-skinned. But many are from the Middle East or Spain or North Africa originally. I don't know. My father and mother were both whiter than me. Jews have much mixed blood, and somehow I came out this way."

"And she's very beautiful," I said with some bite.

"Oh, yes, for sure," he said, showing his embarrassment. "I didn't mean anything by it. It just confused me. I was in Switzerland before I came here. They had a lot of blondes, but so many had dark hair there too. I thought the Swedish were almost all blonde."

"The Swedish are mostly blonde," Michaela explained. "But even they have a lot of dark hair. But Germany and Switzerland are farther south and more mixed. They don't have as many blondes. Some, but not mostly. The Swedish have more blondes for sure."

"So how can Switzerland be mostly dark hair and mostly blonde at the same time?"

I stared at him, trying to figure out what he was talking about.

"You mean the Swiss," Michaela replied to him. She then looked at me with a smirk. "Americans don't know geography, Nathan. No offense. I've been with you so long I almost forgot, but now this happy lad reminds me."

She returned her look at him firmly.

"The people that live in Switzerland are not

Swedish. There is a Sweden and there is a Switzerland. The people living in Switzerland are Swiss and those that live in Sweden are Swedish. Swiss cheese, you know. Not Swedish cheese. Swedish meatballs, you know, not Swiss meatballs. Two different countries."

He showed his confusion.

"My Texas friend here is Jewish also," Michaela said to change the subject. "Blond hair and blue eyes and pale white skin. America is the great melting pot, but Jews had a few thousand years' head start on melting pots. You never know by looking at one. Hitler thought he knew."

"I didn't mean anything by it," the guy repeated uneasily.

"We know you didn't," I said, intervening. "It's hard to explain in twenty-five words or less on a bus to Amsterdam."

"For sure," he replied as he turned back around.

It got darker by the minute as we rode along. The mountains hastened the demise of the sun's rays prematurely.

"Such a shame we cannot see the mountains," Michaela said as we stared out the windows of the bus. "A waste. We can't even see the stars tonight. It is so cloudy and dark."

"Austria was going to be the highlight of the trip for me. But you're right, we don't even get a starry, starry night out of this."

"We must come back this way, Nathan. Someday when we are older."

"That's a comforting thought," I said. "You and me coming back here together. Yes, we must plan to do so. We will do this again, but better."

Michaela and I found a more comfortable sleeping arrangement for our second night on the bus. At first, she lay backward on my lap, but her feet dangled out into the aisle as she did so. After several angles and positions, we settled for our arms embracing and with her head buried into my chest. My head was again on top of hers, but at a more comfortable angle for me.

"Where are we now?" I asked her as I felt her pull herself upright. "It's still dark."

"No idea. But I am dying to use the toilet. The sun is glimmering now on the horizon. Soon it will be up. No mountains. In the distance I see some shadows of mountains."

"Yeah, my bladder is screaming also. I barely drank water all yesterday, but my bladder doesn't care. No mercy. There are people lined up to use the one toilet on the bus. No mercy."

"I see city lights ahead of us. I am glad the sun is not yet fully up. Seeing city lights ahead gives me hope we will stop to let our nature forces survive."

As if on cue, the driver of the bus began speaking on the loudspeakers.

"We will have a rest stop in the next town. If you were asleep, we entered Germany an hour ago. We are in the state of Bavaria. After our stop, this will be the last segment of the journey. Perhaps you see the lights of the city we are approaching. There will be once again a change of drivers. The break will be approximately thirty minutes. Please stay near the bus. We will not have the facilities of a bus stop in this town. You will have to arrange for your own needs at your discretion. Please keep in sight of the bus or you will be left behind."

Michaela and I looked at one another in disbelief.

"So what does that mean?" I asked showing my disapproval. "We're leaving again in thirty minutes, but there is no bus station for us to relieve ourselves. Like we're on our own for whatever needs we have and good luck with that. The one toilet on the bus is always full."

"This is crazy, Nathan. I am sure I will appreciate the adventure one of these days, but right now I am desperate for bladder relief. It was four hours ago that we changed the last driver, but that was at a stop. We could get water and sandwiches and bladder relief. We are entering a town with no such stop. Yes, as you say, good luck, peasants."

We drove several minutes into the town. There were trams for mass transportation within the city. Nowhere was there a bus station or even a restaurant for our needs.

Everyone looked around for a restroom as we disembarked. There was nothing. We were stuck, and that was not going to fly.

The girls were the boldest. I loved Europe for this. Even in our desperate way I could not visualize anyone relieving themselves on the street, but that's what these girls were doing. A fuzzy, see-through glass wall was just in front of where our bus stopped. The girls dropped their drawers, then squatted as they leaned their buttocks to the glass while they went at bladder comfort. Our commotion got notice from passersby on the nearby sidewalks. Did this occur every time the Magic Bus arrived?

"Pressed hams," Michaela said with a snicker. "Look at the flattened buttocks as they support themselves on the glass wall. Pressed hams. The guys are courteous enough to go to the side for their relief. Well, Nathan, I must join the girls here. You've seen me in a natural way already. So *ciao*. We can meet on the bus. I hope you don't need number two. I am glad we didn't eat much."

A long yellow stream formed at the curb on the street near our bus. It seemed so absurdly funny that I got past the disgust quickly.

"Thank God," Michaela said as she sat back next to me on the bus. "As cheap as this ride is, if we had known the fringe benefits—is that the word? Ha!—I am not sure how many of us would have made the journey."

"All of us would," I said with a laugh. "I'm glad we didn't know, but all this is fun in its own way. As long as I don't have to ever do it again."

"*Genau*." She snickered. "Exactly, my friend."

"The last segment of the trip," I said with a sigh. "Another four hours, someone said. I can handle it. We're almost there."

"We are getting the first hostel we come across in Amsterdam," Michaela instructed. "I am so tired. You are comfortable, my love, but I am not sleeping well. It is more like I pass out from exhaustion."

"*Genau*." I mimicked her seemingly favorite German expression. "*Genau*. Right on the money. And I'm not getting up for days, I think."

"I have been to Amsterdam many times," Michaela said. "It is a very youth-oriented city. There is legal prostitution there."

"I have heard that," I said. "And drugs are legal, too. At least marijuana."

"Do you smoke?" she asked me curiously.

"No. I'm not into drugs. I don't even drink much."

"A very sober person," she said with a smile.

"I get high on love."

"I am glad of that. But Nathan, we are in this youth culture capital of Europe, maybe of the world. I have heard that many of the hostels serve a joint with the meal. Is that okay? This exchange. Is that the way to put it? Cultural exchange? We don't have to partake, but we will be in this kind of world now."

"I assumed you had a joint somewhere in your past."

"There is a world out there. I want to be a part of the world, but not get bogged down in a drop-out culture. There is no appeal to indulge in such a culture, but it can be fun to vibe with the natives sometimes. If you manage life well, you grow. Be wise, not foolish."

"When in Rome," I replied.

"Yes, when in Amsterdam, we must indulge in the new age of the hippies. Just not foolishly, I hope. We will be in the mix of this new age, but we do not have to partake."

"*Genau.*"

Chapter 12

I wasn't sure marijuana was harmless, but it sounded non-addictive. I could survive it. The drug, at least. But I was aware it still might open some psychological process in me that succumbed to a new path. Perhaps a dangerous one. I did not become an alcoholic from my first beer or wine and trusted that I would not be lured to the drug culture with my first joint. It was still possible, however, that a previously tabooed culture might suck me in, now that I was opening up to it somewhat by being blatantly around it. I had seen such things happen, including as a Marine with other Marines. I wanted no part of this culture, except to mingle, not indulge. And alcohol had indeed destroyed a lot of lives, even if it didn't mine.

So many from my generation had opted for the hip occult, and I couldn't hide from the culture wars I faced in my youth, had I wanted to. I either believed in my causes or I didn't. So I wanted to be careful but be challenged. To stand up to it. Most of my generation that succumbed to the new ways weren't absorbed by new truths as much as new trends. New truths did exist, but new traps also. One had to grow, or else succumb like a novice in a new religion. The new hip culture was the latest trend to appear, equipped with their own rituals and support mechanisms. A naïve person could remain naively traditional, or naively opt for the new wave. You grow or you don't. Life is for learning. Bring it on. But buyer beware.

I loved traditional America. The old values. Not bigotry, not Jim Crow, nor religious fanaticism, or the scores of other dark elements within our society that challenged our ideals. The mechanisms we had throughout our history to work out our differences enticed me, though. Growing from our mistakes was a virtue and not by accident. It came by design throughout our history. We had everything it took to figure out what was wrong and what to do about it. This was encouraging about my country and its values.

Burning the flag was a trait of much of my generation, as well as much of the drug culture. That action appalled me, but it also made me think. Was I just being old-fashioned, or was there any substance to my views? Could I manage any of the new-age views? In our history, we had to deal with slavery and with who could vote. Even which economic system to implement. The problems just kept coming. But we responded to the challenges well enough that I felt confident we had what it took to grow from anything. The rest was up to me as an individual. If I indulged in the new age while I was in Amsterdam, its de facto capital, would I open myself to chaos from which I might not recover, or would this be a rewarding experience from which I learned and grew? An experience worthy to take back with me to Texas and further into adulthood.

To experience Amsterdam with Michaela added to the allure of this new-age adventure. This was going to be fun, I decided. She was as game as I was, but with more experience in this realm. She took it in stride. Adaptability is a survivor's trait. She was a survivor of the first realm.

As we walked the streets of Amsterdam looking for a hostel, the impact of the new age hit us right in the face. Prostitutes solicited our attention as we passed by. Not just by calling out to us, but by exposing key portions of their anatomy as advertisement. It made Las Vegas appear like a night club in comparison. With its water canals for streets, Amsterdam combined a touch of classical Venice with its bawdiness.

"Don't they know I brought my own?" I chided Michaela amidst the sexual solicitations.

"I am the one that speaks German. A bit of Dutch in the mix. I can hear for whom they call out. What makes you think they want just you?"

I let out a laugh.

"I'm a bit provincial, Michaela. Yeah, what made me think this was all about me?"

"It is fun for now, but it gets old soon, Nathan. I am glad you are experiencing this. As part of an education for a backpacker. But who wants to live this way? Go to the circus called the redlight district of Amsterdam, but then go home. That's what this means to me. Let's find our hostel, and I don't want it to be here. I want a bit of peace. The freaks at the hostel will be enough of a show. Something else to experience with you. But then I am ready to go home. I want to show you my home in provincial Germany."

She looked at me, studying my face.

"How long will you stay in Europe do you think? How long do you think you will spend with me before going back to Texas?"

"I don't really know. I'm living day to day. First let's get you home. We'll see what we do together, and

I'll make arrangements to go home when you're settled."

"I don't have time to travel around Europe with you. I must prepare for my studies again. I want to introduce you to my mother. She is a widow now. Since two years ago. I want you to visit my father's grave when we get back, to share my father with you. He will be happy to know I have fallen in love with a Jew, after all he went through because he was a Jew. And my sister and her husband live in the same town as my mother. We will visit them. They are preparing to live in Africa soon. He is a doctor. He has a job in Johannesburg for a year. That is exciting to me. I want to live in Africa someday, but not really in South Africa with its apartheid. Because of the British Empire, so much of Africa speaks English, thank goodness. Also French because of French and Belgian colonies. So I hope I can find a job somewhere."

She looked at me pointedly. "I hope you can go with me to Africa. Or meet me there later. I know you must study. As do I. But somewhere I hope we can meet in Africa. Think about it. We haven't talked about our future. Only vaguely. Me coming to study in Texas. Finishing our studies. Finding a job afterwards. But soon, Nathan, we will be apart for a while. I don't like this part of us. The separation approaching us. While we are apart, however, this will tell us how we feel. We must reflect. Were they just holiday feelings? The only thing good about being apart is how we feel about each other while we are apart. Even knowing we plan to see each other again in Texas. In your environment. While separate, we can reflect on our true feelings."

I did want to know if we were experiencing the real thing. It seemed like we were, but what if it was the holiday spirit playing games with us? And if these feelings now were real, what were we going to do with them? She was from Germany and I was going back to Texas. Even if she came to Texas, what then? This was so complicated. It made me nervous.

We walked several more blocks to make sure we were far from the red-light district. It was a nice walk and showed a more promising part of Amsterdam. The not so touristic part with cafes, shops, and other businesses strewn along the canals of the city.

"There, Nathan," Michaela said as she stared straight ahead. "A sign saying hostel. Not the big international chain. Those are nice, but I am glad we found a more local one." She looked at me with a twinkle in her eye. "This one will be more youth oriented. And all that it implies."

I didn't respond. I welcomed any chance of a surprise.

"Are you looking to share a room or prefer the dormitory arrangement?" the clerk asked us as we checked in.

I let Michaela do the talking, not wanting her to feel pressured.

"A room, please," she replied matter-of-factly.

That response made me happy. The clerk handed her the key, then directed us to where the room was.

"We shower, first thing," she ordered as we placed our backpacks on the bed in our room.

"The bed is so narrow," I remarked. "It is one and a half wide, not even a double."

She looked at me to wink.

"Good, Nathan. Very cozy, don't you think?"

"The small bed requires some snuggling arrangements," I said with a smirk.

"*Genau*."

"*Genau*," I seconded.

"The shower room is mixed gender. No choice like in Nicosia. Only one shower room here. I read about it on the door as we entered. To let everyone know what to expect in this place. And it does serve a joint for breakfast, the same notice said. So, my dear, experience our quaint youth center called Amsterdam. Something to tell the grandchildren someday when they brag about how hip they are. We will have stories of our own to tell them."

"So we shower together this time, I take it, Michaela. Not that we didn't already at the waterfall. But together publicly this time. Our debut as lovers in the mega hipdom."

At first Michaela and I had the shower to ourselves. Soon two other couples joined us. They thought nothing of disrobing in front of us. One big happy naked family, we were. Michaela and I scrubbed each other down as did the other couples. One couple, however, made a big to-do out of fondling and kissing. It seemed like a show to me, but entertaining.

I loved Amsterdam.

Chapter 13

"Now that we know each other better," I said in a low voice as we lay in bed in our hostel room, "I want to talk about something."

"Nathan, we cannot get married. I love you, but do not spoil it now, please. You know we can't trust our feelings yet. I know they are real, but there is so much to work out first. Not just about our relationship, but our own separate lives. Please understand this. Please know that I love you, and the happiest joy I could imagine is spending the rest of our lives together, but we just are not to a level yet to trust anything about us. To trust ourselves, I mean. We are living some honeymoon right now."

"Well," I replied with a chuckle, "I guess that saves me the trouble of not asking you to marry me. I'm not ready to marry yet either. Remember this conversation. Thanks for rejecting my proposal to you that I wasn't going to make. Yeah, I'm glad us not getting married is your idea. I think. So there."

She rubbed my cheek affectionately.

"Okay," she said with a sigh. "Maybe I should be hurt, but I'm not. It's a relief then to not think of marriage right now. I don't want to hurt you. There is an appeal to the idea of living forever by the waterfall in Cyprus. Or on some glorious beach somewhere with you. But I am nervous about my life. And now, meeting the love of my life puts a pressure on me I am not prepared for. I need to graduate. First priorities first. And I want to go to Africa. I want to find my place in life, except part of the finding is how I have found you."

"God, Michaela, stop. Now, son-of-a-gun, I want to marry you after all. Reject me again and maybe I'll want you even more."

"Are you trying to trick me, Nathan? Seriously, I love you so deeply. I'm just not ready for a commitment. Not a definite one anyway. No vows of any sort yet, you know. Are you trying to trick me into wanting this? I don't want to want it. Let me just live with the happiness we have found for a bit longer."

"Okay, now that that's settled, let's talk about what I really wanted to bring up before you spurned the marriage proposal I wasn't going to give. What I really wanted to talk about is your father. How he was a Jew in Nazi Germany. How did he survive, Michaela? I wanted to know even in Israel on the kibbutz. But you were so guarded about it. I understand. Who wants to open such a deep wound? But now, maybe we can talk about some of this, if you don't mind? Is it okay? I have never met a survivor of the holocaust. I've seen documentaries, but never met anyone. So I can't ask your father. He has passed on, but maybe you can talk to me some about it. Maybe you trust me enough. Is it okay?"

"Oh, Nathan," she said with a moan. "I want to talk with you about this. To honor you as the first I've ever told. I seldom even talk with my mother about this. Seldom anything before, with my father. I don't know so much. But what I do know wants to come out. To talk to someone. Israel would have been a place to talk to someone, but I was never comfortable even there. It felt awkward, and I never found a way with anyone. It surprised me."

"If it's too hard, I understand. I don't want to poke at old scars."

"I know. I wondered sometimes if I would be able to talk to you about it. Just because we are so in love doesn't mean I can talk about it. I feel like I am betraying our family secret."

"I understand. I do. I don't want to put you on the spot."

Michaela turned away from me onto her side, facing the door of our hostel room. The shadow of her figure in the dark seemed brooding and mysterious.

"We are in Amsterdam," she said just above a whisper. "Anne Frank. She was born in Frankfurt, but her family moved to Amsterdam after the Nazis took over Frankfurt. But then they took over Amsterdam too."

Michaela turned back toward me.

"Yes, Nathan, I need to talk to you about my father. About my father's situation when the Nazis took over Germany. There is much I do not know. It was hard for my parents to say anything. Even after the war there were still dangers. It was best to just move on with our lives. We did not talk much about it, but my parents did want me to know things. I have not told anyone. It was such a dark time when my parents lived this. They wanted to protect me. Now that it is time to talk to someone, I don't know how. But I can and I will. I know just enough to feel the Nazi horror, and that is all I can handle. To be aware. '*Never again*' is what everyone says about all this. I know enough to vow '*never again.*' And then I cannot handle anymore."

"Where were they then? Your parents. Where were

they geographically?"

"Where I lived growing up. A small village a few minutes from Frankfurt called Moerfelden. My father was Jewish. Every town and village needs stores and banks and doctors and lawyers. So there were Jews to supply needs for these villages. Not just Jews supplied such services, but these are Jewish specialties."

"What did your father do? Or his family?"

"Watches and jewelry. Typical, I know. I have a bite in me to answer that question. Not because of you. I don't mind that you asked me. You're even Jewish and face many of the same stereotypes. But when stereotypes get you killed, that is more than any petty bigotry. Shylocks or hook noses or blood libels. All these images and slanders of the Jews. Whatever makes someone an enemy in some tribal mindset of mankind. These are not petty and boring stereotypes against us to laugh off or mock. These stereotypes make you the cesspool of society to so many. Or 'vermin' as Herr Hitler called us."

"Are you okay, Michaela? I don't need to know these things."

"I need to tell you now, Nathan. Especially because you are Jewish. You are American, but the stigma of being a Jew did not escape America. Even if it was not the same stigma like here in Germany or so much of Europe. Much of the New World dream was there for Jews in this new laboratory of enlightenment called America. But America also created Old World problems of their own. Genocides against the Indians occurred, I am aware. There were also hate groups in America similar to here. But there was a new spirit also in America. A chance to start again. Somehow a dream to make right all these wrongs. You had your own problems, but also a new vision to lead you. So I need a New World Jew to know what you left behind by landing on Plymouth Rock. I need to tell you some of what my parents lived when they were young here."

She placed her head on my shoulder. A new chapter in our relationship was developing that I welcomed. She stroked my neck with her hand for a moment, as if in thought with how to begin. Trust. She trusted me. I was special to her.

"Even before *Kristallnacht*, the Jews were feeling pressure. I am sure you know what Kristallnacht is. The night of broken glass, in English. November ninth and tenth in 1938. The last of anything Jewish was stripped from Germany. Our shops looted, synagogues destroyed. Never to vote again or be seen as human again. Hatred. Hatred is not even the correct word. There is no word for all that went on. We were a people that had been in central Europe since the Roman Empire. But scattered. Strangers in a strange land. So how did we come to be outcasts in the mid-twentieth century after millennia living and assimilating in our new homes? Part of the propaganda spewed out about us was how we were a separate people. Loyal to no one except ourselves. That we contributed nothing, that we refused to protect our fellow Germans during times of war and invasion."

"It's hard to believe that people can believe such lies. On a massive scale, I mean. I know it happens all the time, but as I listen, it's so hard to picture."

"Yes, I know, Nathan. And arguments against these lies were brought out during this vitriol. The fact is, more Jews in Germany, per capita, fought in World War I, Nathan, the most recent war before World War II, than members of the general population. But truth was suppressed just as the scientific genius of Einstein and Freud was suppressed. Two brilliant German Jews were denied recognition by the Nazis. Why have the truth when there can be hatred? So here was my father brought up in such diatribe. All he had to be was Jewish to be condemned to death. Nothing else. Just being Jewish got you killed after Kristallnacht. Especially with the ordained 'final solution' as an official policy beginning in 1940."

She raised on her arm to look at me more directly, in the eyes. I studied her in the dark as she did so. I could see and feel her intensity.

"One day he was not allowed to go to school with his friends anymore. He wasn't German anymore, but an invader. A polluter. Scum. He told me that was when he really began to feel like a Jew. He was only vaguely aware until then that he was Jewish. Some Jews were Catholic after conversion, some atheists, some Lutheran, while some were still practicing Judaism. Being a Jew meant more than just being a religious person of the Jewish faith. Being a Jew was a racial element. A Jew was a Jew, whoever decided. And now being Jewish meant not being German. Of not ever being German."

She looked past me, as if talking to the wall.

"His parents began to teach him school courses at home. He was due to graduate, but now he could only learn for the sake of knowledge. He would be considered unskilled even with this knowledge because he did not graduate from the local German schools. Jewish shops were being smashed in the cities. Many Jews were leaving Germany by then. One day soldiers came."

"Wait, Michaela. I've heard stories like this before. If you are talking about after Kristallnacht, why hadn't

101

your parents already left?"

"Because no one could really believe the insanity would persist. Everyone was fearful of a pogrom. Jews always had to know such could happen. But there had been so much hope in post-enlightenment Europe. Germany especially seemed to be on some glorious path. Education, science, prosperity. Here comes Hitler, but surely he would be gone soon. He took advantage of a desperate economic and political situation after World War I, and then the depression. But everyone was certain Germany was too progressive now to go back to the Dark Ages. That is how people thought at the time. Surely this will be over soon. Hitler brought a pride of being German again. But soon the madness would be gone that came with this pride."

"Yes, I have heard all of this. But now as you tell the story, it hits home with more reality."

"One day the soldiers came," she continued. "His mother, my grandmother, hid my father in the basement, just to be safe. There was a tunnel in the basement. It went to a shed they had. She told him to go through this tunnel to the shed. They used this tunnel many times, and he was familiar with it. From the shed, my father saw the soldiers take my grandparents away. He waited an hour after they left. It was dark by then, and he ran the kilometer to my grandmother's house—my mother's mother, you know. They were Christian and friends of ours. But anymore, how could you really know if anyone could be trusted? He had to try."

"It could have meant death to hide a Jew," I mused. "Why would they do this? Even if they knew his family beforehand, so many would not risk their lives to hide a Jew."

"And so many betrayed their Jewish friends willingly anyway, Nathan. Hitler understood human nature. So many Germans tolerated the Jews more than they accepted them. Somehow the Jews were still strangers in a strange land. Foreigners in their own homeland."

"I remember reading about the Dreyfuss affair in France," I commented.

"Yes, the Jewish lieutenant in the French Army just before the turn of the century."

"After the Age of Enlightenment, the Jews were so hopeful. Surely now the world was maturing. Yes, science, education, the world getting smaller with all the exploration. But then there was a scandal and the late-nineteenth-century French needed a scapegoat. Enlightenment went right out the window. And the Jew Dreyfuss was found guilty of treason."

"Security was never there for the Jew, Nathan. It never is anywhere. I feel secure in Germany now, but I am not naïve. I know that someday, somewhere, some person or group is going to need to blame the Jews again."

"With the trial of Lieutenant Dreyfuss," I related from my own learning while growing up, "everyone realized the need for a Jewish homeland again. A place for Jews to grow together and protect themselves."

"The Zionist movement began from all of this. But back to my father, Nathan. That is the background, and now my father was an orphan. He was sixteen then. A man. A boy still somewhat, but a man. And the family of my mother took pity. They barely knew one another. Friends, but not close friends. They didn't care so much for Jews either. But this was insane, they decided. All that was happening now after Kristallnacht. And Kristallnacht was after the *Night of the Longknives*. You know when Hitler went on his purges. Not just of Jews or the political opposition, but anyone that might present a threat. He even got rid of his own private army that helped get him all his power. This was to assure the support of the German regular army. He became entrenched in power. But it wasn't until three years later with Kristallnacht that he concentrated on the Jewish problem. There was harassment before Kristallnacht, and my father and his parents survived that, and so hoped to survive again. But it became obvious that worse was coming. There would be no going back to the good old days, or even the days of uneasy peace. After Kristallnacht would come some final solution like in 1940."

"So you said he was an orphan. This would have been before Auschwitz. What happened to his parents?"

"He never found out. They were obviously sent to some concentration camp. A resettlement at first, perhaps. I don't know. But there was nothing my father could find out about them. If they survived, he would have known. If they escaped, they would have found him after the war. So we can use our imagination. That is all I know. Not so much. Just that my father successfully hid in the attic of my maternal grandmother's house. It also had a secret room. It wasn't really a secret room. It was a storage room, but it was sealed up to protect him. They made a secret passage from a closet in the next room."

"If the Nazis had won the war, he would still be there in that room then," I thought aloud.

"I'm sure he would have been captured before that. The Nazis quit looking soon. At my mother's house, I mean. And the war started soon after that. I am sure he was a burden, but by then he and my mother were very much in love. Nature doesn't care about your politics. I don't really know what my grandparents thought of this, but they were already in danger. They had to go along to survive, and I heard they liked my father. Amazing as it is, everyone survived."

"Except Hitler."

"*Genau.* I don't really believe in Hell, Nathan. But if it turns out there is one, well. I do hope for some accountability about him. Even if not Hell. Hell is too permanent."

"I see these documentaries of the prison camps. Dachau and all. Of Hitler's rise to power. It kind of makes sense how it happened. Except that it never will make sense to me. I am sure I am able to be fooled and perhaps even be led by some pied piper, but it still doesn't make sense."

"You would never be so fooled, Nathan. You are too sincere. You really look for answers. We all follow some charlatan. Some phony. A politician, a religious imposter, or these days some rock-and-roll star. But to join a demonic cult. you wouldn't fall for that."

"I saw the movie *Cabaret*, Michaela. It may be my favorite movie."

"Yes, I love that movie also. Very realistic. It does show how it could happen. Just one day, there you are. Believing in the great cause."

"What made me think it could happen to me was the scene where that little Nazi boy at the outdoor restaurant got up to sing."

"Oh, yes, that was a very inspiring scene. It was a *Biergarten* actually. Like a restaurant, but mostly to sit

Larry Farmer

and enjoy socially, with wine and beer and also some food while you relax."

"I was more than inspired. I could feel it. I love history, for one thing, and have studied about prewar Germany and Hitler's rise. I even read *Mein Kampf*. My mother is a history teacher and of course knows about those days. My dad fought in the war against the Nazis. But I watched that crowd in the Biergarten scene in *Cabaret* get up and sing fervently with that Nazi boy. Their time had come. The Nazis were now unstoppable. From out of nowhere, suddenly unstoppable. And I wanted to get up from my seat at that movie house and sing with them. Not give the Nazi salute, but I could feel this spirit and determination. The total devotion. Tomorrow belongs to me, Michaela. So I can conceive about getting caught up in the Germany of that time. It served a purpose at first. I pictured it all as I studied about it through the years. Then the movie got it through. You are living day by day, and at first the Nazis seemed the goons they were. But the best way to lose a war is to underestimate your opponent. The whole world underestimated the Nazis. They were brilliant goons and focused. The movie led us through one day at a time. Then, in perfect synchronization, at that Biergarten, as if a magic wand appeared, this Nazi boy gets up out of his seat and starts singing *Tomorrow Belongs to Me*. I loved it. It moved me. It was perfect. *No one is going to treat us this way anymore, bad old world. We're not going to take it. Tomorrow belongs to me and Germany is on the rise. Germany is capable, Germany is ordained.* I loved it. It took reminding myself of the rest of the story to snap me out of my trance."

"I am too German to be swept away with this

106

adulation, Nathan. And too Jewish. It was personal to me as I watched the movie and that scene. I lived the horror, or at least the aftermath. My father lived it literally and had to survive it. I can understand, I guess, why that Nazi boy had his moment. That song was originally written by two Jews, you know. The movie improvised the words for the scene, but the spirit was Jewish. Sorry, Herr Hitler. The Jews weren't trying to take over the world when they wrote it. The Nazi version had exactly that in mind. To take over the world. Typical somehow. Project your own guilt on the one you accuse."

"I agree, Michaela. But I can't just condemn it. Part of getting past things is to understand. I am glad I got some understanding out of that scene, because it reinforced my own '*never again*.' It made me appreciate being a Jew, and I am especially grateful for that. I love being assimilated. Being American. Being a Texan and a Marine. All these things. But I am a Jew. Born a Jew, but now a Jew by choice, especially. And I don't mean the religion, but the people. It was one of the reasons I went to Israel when I did. I wanted to find my Jewish self. Israel got that through to me. I am so much a Jew now. And tomorrow belongs to me."

"Yes, Nathan, I understand that. That is how I feel. Before, I identified as a Jew because of my father. But Israel made me want to be a Jew because that is what I am. That is the importance of Israel. Not just a refuge for victimized Jews. It is for the realization of what being a Jew is. I may never go back to Israel. But I know I will always be a Jew. One of the tribe."

Chapter 14

"Where we are going now is near Switzerland," Michaela said as we looked out from the train into the German countryside. "That is where you should go first after you leave me to travel. I have an apartment in the town Freiburg. I lived with a friend before, and she is waiting on me. I left my things with her. The things I use and wear as a student, I mean. Her family owns a cottage in the town where we are going. Freiburg is a charming place near France as well as Switzerland, not far from the Rhine River."

"This is going to be goodbye for us. I've dreaded it."

"I also regret this goodbye. We knew it would arrive, and here it is. I get to focus on my studies and that will help me get past the loneliness. I love my studies. I love being a student. So I will miss you, but I will have a productive routine to rely on. You will be all right too, my dear. We managed to get you a Eurorail Pass. That is three weeks of first-class travel on most any train in Europe. We are sleeping on the train now as we travel all night from Amsterdam, but you will still have over two weeks remaining when you travel on your own. You will forget you ever met me soon enough."

I thought to chastise her for such a callous remark. First-class travel on luxurious trains would be my distraction, however, just like her studies would be for her. Rome, Paris, Vienna, Zurich, and other cities would keep me occupied, for sure. I loved Europe and would surely love it even more by the time I went home to my own studies.

"Don't send post cards, Nathan," she teased me. "Don't be so bourgeois. Enjoy, but be the vagabond I fell in love with. Rugged and carefree. Forget about me. It will even be a test of our feelings."

"I'll wonder just how snug you are with your studies." I stared at her for emphasis. "And your friends."

"Friends? What friends? Do you mean male friends?"

"You know what I'm talking about. Out of sight and out of mind we say back home. You won't be looking for a boyfriend, but nature is still alive and kicking."

"And so are your hormones. You will be missing me, but you will be seeing sexy women everywhere you go. Not to mention distractions like the Roman Colosseum, and the Eiffel Tower, as well as beautiful lakes and mountains. So little time then for memories of me. Are you going to Scandinavia? You will need a train. So you have Eurorail. That is free train travel for you. You should use it there. There are vast hinterlands in these countries."

"Free," I scoffed. "I paid plenty for the Eurorail Pass. And we're using up two days of it getting you back to southern Germany. To this town Freiburg."

"But it is cheap for all you get to see. One price for a vast continent. You should travel with it every day. That is another reason you cannot stay with me long in Freiburg. You should be on the train. Even sleep on the train. If you travel first class, you will have compartments to yourself at night quite often. Just pull out the seats and they become like beds. It's wonderful.

Made for tourists. We don't do this for ourselves. It is an enticement to get American dollars or Arab oil money into our economy. To sucker you here with an allure of vast and cheap travel. Anyway, you will forget all about me very soon."

I had no idea all I would be feeling once we separated. I was glad she had her focus on school while I would be seeing new worlds of my choosing. But forgetting her seemed impossible.

"Yes, Michaela, it will be a test for us, won't it?"

"We are two different people from two different worlds, Nathan. Both of us Westerners and Jews, but nothing else in common. It will be a test indeed. Were we just now on holiday together in a hormonal festival, or did we really fall in love with one another? I don't even want to think of this as a test. We love each other or we don't. We work things out about us or we move on. Good luck, *monsieur*."

I nodded my head. It sounded good, but it didn't feel very reassuring.

Chapter 15

I was impressed with her student habitat in Freiburg, a charming modernized old German city. Everything looked so clean and prosperous.

"I love traveling, Nathan, and I loved living in Israel. But it is so good to be home. My real home is Frankfurt, a suburb, but Freiburg is all mine now. My own version of home, student that I am. Perfect location. Near Switzerland and France. A couple of hours from either. It is wonderful. And such a pleasant old city. I live in a part of Freiburg that students like. It is a section called Wiehre."

"I've heard of the German miracle. You can't keep a good man down, as they say. It got smacked by losing the Great War, then the devastating Depression. Then a military dictatorship, then losing another devastating war, and now, pow, here you are again. And an ally with America thrown in. We're even friends now."

"Yes, Nathan, you are correct. It is exciting to be German. And we are protected by the mighty America. We are not even allowed too strong a military from our evil past. So you get to protect us from ourselves. Pay the bill and pay us some rent as part of the bargain. For your occupying us with your protective military might against the Communist threat next door. We don't even have to fight the bad guys. America does it for us. We have won the lotto after losing a terrible war. Life is full

Larry Farmer

of paradox, is it not?"

"And you did all this miracle in not even thirty years," I praised.

"I am glad you admire us. I want to share with you my Germany. This cottage is small here, Nathan. My roommate is gone right now. School doesn't start until next week, and she is in Paris until then. These are old wooden houses here that mostly students live in, but they are sturdy. All the conveniences. I love it here."

She walked over to her bed.

"I have a spare mattress in a closet. The mattress is made of sponge. For guests such as you. We will unroll it and lay it next to my bed mattress and make do with the awkward sleeping arrangement. My bed mattress is thicker than the sponge mattress, but we can still snuggle with one another if I put both on the floor. We are backpackers and survivors. This is nothing compared with sleeping in cornfields and sunflower patches."

"*Genau,*" I said with a smirk.

"Come now, Nathan. Let me show you my town. You will love Freiburg. Maybe you will want to attend my university while I go to yours in Texas."

She grabbed me by the hand and led me to her car.

"I'll show you some of the sights, Nathan," she said while getting in. "That's if you can fit into my roller skate of a car. It's a mini. We have small cars in Europe compared to America. And students such as me have the smallest. The car roof curves upward quite a bit. Just in case some Goliath like you tries to ride. It will be a squeeze, and you can't spread out your legs very much, but we won't drive very far. I just want to point out some things. You'll be leaving in a day. I don't want you to waste your Eurorail Pass. You have just over two weeks

112

left on it."

Her car was indeed small. Somehow I fit.

"I want to spend tomorrow with you, Michaela," I explained as she drove into the city center. "I can leave first thing on the day after. But let me feel a bit familiar with you in your environment."

"Fair enough, *Schatz*. I can't believe we went straight through from Frankfurt to here. I wanted to take you to see my mother. She lives near the *Flughafen*. You know, the airport. But we had an express train to Basel, which stopped in Freiburg, and I needed to get back here. I have school soon and must prepare. But we should have spent the night with my mother. Just to meet her. Now I worry you may never get the chance."

I studied her. What did she mean by that? She seemed to pick up on my concern.

"We should never put off when we have the chance to do something now," she explained. "The train stopped at the Flughafen. My mother lives in the next village. It was a wasted opportunity. Now tomorrow you are off again on your own. It's of no concern, really. It's not so important to meet my mother or see my hometown. Just a missed opportunity. I wish we had prepared better. When you come back here, we don't know if I will have time to go back to my home. That's all I was thinking. I hope it makes sense to you."

I felt satisfied with her answer.

"Nathan," she continued, "I want you to enjoy yourself. I expect you to miss me. But you will be seeing so many wonderful sights. Arrange your travels to come back here, and I will make time for you from my studies. You must be patient with my circumstances. But we will be together, and I will drive you to Frankfurt to the

Flughafen when you fly back to Texas. When I send you back to America, we will spend your last night at my mother's in Moerfelden right next to the airport. It is sad to think about but also exciting."

"I would love to meet your mother."

"I am coming to Texas," she said with a chirp. "I very much look forward to this. I will live with that joy more than the melancholy of our separation. We have a future still. We don't have to make any other plans than these simple ones now. And that's what I want. No more plans. Just live day by day and let life decide things."

"I can let life decide for us, Michaela. But Mother Nature is a tyrant about our feelings."

"Shush, *Mein Schatz*. Be still. I am coming in a few months to see you and live with you in Texas. That is enough for now. I may even be there by Christmas. Before your school starts next year in the spring semester. You can find us a place to stay while waiting on me. Think of this. Think of us together in Texas."

She looked over at me, but I kept looking straight ahead.

"We arrive now at the marketplace, Nathan. I will park here and show you. Just to familiarize you. The university here is famous. And like your Harvard. Did you know I was so smart as to go to our version of Harvard?"

"I'm not surprised, Michaela. Good."

"Freiburg is one of the original universities in Germany. The oldest in what is now Germany itself. Since 1457, Nathan. That is before Columbus discovered the New World. Our university here was founded by the Hapsburg dynasty. I know that is Austrian, but back then it was the dominant German *reich*, or kingdom. And the

University of Freiburg was the second university founded by this kingdom. Their capital was Vienna. Only the University of Vienna itself is older than our university here. The German tribes were still so divided. What is now Austria was the center of power for much of these German tribes. It was Austria that began establishing universities. I am bragging now of the world where I belong. All this history. There was a Freiburg University before there was a Harvard and even before there was a known New World. I want you to appreciate me. I will show you parts of the university tomorrow. Only a bit. Just for you to know you have seen me in my glory. Then you will be on your way. First travel a bit of Europe, then back to Texas and wait for me."

Chapter 16

Michaela and I were in our phase two, I decided as I rode the train into Switzerland after leaving Freiburg. Being apart now was as pronounced as the times we shared together.

I loved her. I already knew that, but it was more apparent now that we were separated. I loved the pain I felt from being away from her. This was real, the pain said to me. I cherished it for that.

The Swiss customs agent entered the train just before we crossed the Rhine River into the city of Basel. The Rhine was one of the few rivers in Europe I knew, but Switzerland was another country for me. They may as well have been fairy tales before. Now I was living them.

The Rhine makes Basel the one port city in landlocked Switzerland, as it links it to the North Sea. I considered finding a room and enjoying myself in my first Swiss city, but there were still a few hours of daylight remaining, and I felt the pressure to use my Eurorail Pass. There was so much I hoped to see with barely two weeks to enjoy it.

Basel was significant to me, however, as a Jew. I departed the train to check out tourist information.

"Yes," the guide informed me, "Hotel Les Trois Rois is not so far. I will mark it on a city map for you."

Searching out the hotel where Theodore Herzl held

the first Zionist Congress back in the late nineteenth century was important to me. The devotion I held from my renewed Jewishness was pounding inside me. Here I was in Basel as the full impact hit. It was all in front of me now. How far should I carry this, I wondered? I was still in a hurry, and I had seen so many historic Jewish sites in Israel, I decided not to dwell. But I had to at least gawk, take a picture, and feel the awe.

As I focused my reverence toward the hotel, I began to get emotional. I was proud to be Jewish, but now it seemed the most cherished aspect of me. These men who planned the Zionist movement in the building just in front of me seemed biblically significant somehow. The Jews had been the scattered outcasts of history forever. And I could feel the determination they must have felt to turn this stigma around.

A picture was enough of a memento, I determined. This hotel would be my entire memory of Basel. I felt as part of the tribe of Zion that vowed, "Tomorrow Belongs to Me."

With my mission accomplished, I rushed back to the train station. The next express left within the hour.

Switzerland compares to Connecticut in size. If I traveled much in it, I would run out of country quickly. After hearing so much about its beauty, I determined I wanted to experience a bit of it firsthand. And not just from a train window.

The Swiss capital of Bern was barely an hour away. Part of the Alps run through this province. The Bernese Alps they call them. That meant mountains were part of the tour. I would spend the night in Bern then, to get my bearings and decide which mountains I wanted to see the most. Even if it meant not traveling the train for a day or two and wasting my Eurorail for that period. Mountains trumped free travel easily.

There were only hills and meadows on the way to Bern from Basel, but even they were breathtaking, so green and pristine.

As the train rolled into the city of Bern, I saw old stone houses, a bustling river, stone streets, a medieval clock tower, and snow-capped mountains towering in the background. Every inch of Switzerland got more gorgeous as I passed farther into it. I suspected my euphoria was just beginning.

Where was Michaela now in all of this? Not sharing Basel was already unbearable for me. Bern demanded a soulmate. Emotions were exploding, and I had nowhere to put them with her gone. I would never do this again. I would never feel anything without her being with me.

"Go to the marketplace," a woman at a tobacco stand suggested to me as I asked for directions. "After you leave the *Bahnhof* turn to the left. *Bahnhof* means train station. Turn left and there will be street musicians. You will see many *bratwurst* stands. *Bratwurst* is a German type of sausage, much like what you call a hot dog, but so much better. And there are many Turkish *gyro* booths also. A *gyro*, some say a *Euro*, are shavings of beef and lamb wrapped in flat bread. The bread is called Pita bread. Shaped like a small pizza crust. There are booths in the marketplace that sell clothes and jewelry. All in front of our Parliament building. Bern is the national capital, and perhaps you know this. But we are a true confederacy here. Bern is not the dictator of Switzerland. It is merely the capital city of the country. Switzerland is made up of Cantons, like a county in America. Each Canton has more power in running their lives than Bern has as the capital of the country. Bern simply deals with treaties, currency, and running the military. Whatever a province or Canton does not handle, Bern handles. It coordinates stability for the country. Enjoy. Switzerland is a marvelous place. But expensive. You may enjoy the sites more than the shops."

"Thank you," I said with a broad smile. I was charmed by her explanation.

"Speak a bit of the local dialect, *bitte*," she instructed further. "*Bitte* means please, but also thank you. A polite response to give someone, in other words. So instead of saying thank you, you must say *bitte*. But better than *bitte* is *merci*."

"I thought *merci* was thank you in French," I replied.

"Very good," she answered. "You will do nicely here. Switzerland, for as small as she is, has four national languages. German is the main language. Bern, Basel, Zurich, St. Gallen, and most of the country speak German, but each with their own dialect. But Geneva and Lausanne speak French. The Tessin region in the south speaks Italian, and St. Moritz, maybe you know this town from the skiing, speaks an old Latin dialect called Romanish. So try to learn a few polite words to feel a part of us. *Ciao*."

"*Merci*," I answered her.

I adored Switzerland already, more than any place so far except Israel, and because of the people as much as the scenery.

Across the street from the *Bahnhof* was a bank. That seemed appropriate somehow. Was I stereotyping? There was much to stereotype about this small country. It was famous for banks, cheese, watches, jewelry, chocolate, and mountains.

Turn left, I reminded myself. As I walked, I marveled once again at how clean everything was. It had old-country charm as well.

Quickly, I came upon the large clock tower I had seen before, from the train. *Zytglogge* they called it. There were two hands, as usual. However, these were full-length hands that took up the entire diameter of the face of the clock. One hand was bigger and fancier at its ends. I assumed this made it the hour hand.

A tunnel not much larger than a car width passed through the base of the Zytglogge. A streetcar track ran through this tunnel. Bern was priceless art called a city.

A large plaza area greeted me on the other side of the tunnel, with more shops of food, jewelry, supermarkets, records, and candy. The candy got my attention the most. I wanted Swiss chocolate immediately. I wasn't hungry, but that made no difference.

I swooned as I saw all the choices in the glass counters. Not just chocolate, but pastry. I had no idea if the lady behind the counter spoke English. I pointed at the darkest and thickest pieces of fudge and cakes that I saw.

I knew just enough German numbers to get her the amount of money needed for my feast. I opened my backpack to put the small paper sack of goodies into it, but pulled out a piece of cake to nibble on before I did so.

It was a bright sunny day, and the Bernese Alps shone brilliantly as I walked farther into the market area. I could hear a street musician nearby, but the snowcapped peaks behind the Parliament building captured my attention the most. As charmed as I was by

Bern, I quickly began to wonder what I was doing here. The sun was making its way through the sky. It was afternoon and, happily, in the summertime. That was good not just for the warmth in the air, but the sun still had a ways to go before it reached the horizon behind those mountains.

I had a Eurorail Pass that was burning daylight. Suddenly, that was all that mattered to me. The ride into Bern and the few blocks I walked of the city's center was enough, I decided. As limited as my endeavor was into this gorgeous Swiss city, I decided Bern was the city I loved most in the entire world. But those mountains were calling me, like some *Bali Hai.*

Chapter 17

"Grindelwald," the woman at the information booth in the train station recommended. She then pointed to a track nearby. "You must take that train. Hurry now, as it is preparing to leave. Americans love Interlaken the most, but I promise you, Grindelwald will be your favorite memory of Switzerland."

Every mile I traveled only got more beautiful. Soon I was in the mountains. I wondered if there were any ugly parts of Switzerland. Or even any average parts.

Switzerland was more than clean. It was immaculate. Not just without litter or debris, but as if manicured by guardian angels. The farms also—manmade manicured plots of land to go with Mother Nature's.

The sun shone brilliantly as the train pulled into the Alpen village called Grindelwald. The snowcapped mountains towering above the valley reflected a panoramic spotlight to guide us. Farther and farther into the valley they led us.

Eurorail or not, I would spend the night here rather than on the train. I would not pass up this mountainous wonder. I could not imagine a more scenic place on the face of the earth. Not the Himalayas nor Hawaii could beat this beauty, I was sure.

"*First*," the clerk behind the desk of the youth hostel said to me. "It is spelled like the English word 'first.' But in German it is pronounced *fierst*. Like fierce but with a t sound at the end. First is the mountain that towers just above us here. There is a cable car that takes you most of the way up. That is the most scenic spot. You can even stop along the way and continue on later with the same ticket."

"*Fierst*, you say? Can you write it for me?"

"No need," he replied. "It is spelled like the English number one. Not one itself, but first. Just like I said, like first, like the number one. Such as first, second, third. That is the spelling. First. But it is pronounced with the vowel i in the word sounding like a long e."

He studied me to see if I grasped what he said.

"Feeerrsst," he said exaggerating the sounds. "Go to First and have a lunch there or something. You don't have to climb the mountainsides. If you are a tourist I would not climb alone. Something may happen and there would be no help for you. But get off the cable car and go out to the hillside by the terminal. It is even more breathtaking than what you see here in the valley. You will be near the mountain peaks and can see across the valley and below. It is wonderful. The highlight of your entire trip, I can promise you this much."

The seat on the cable car was open air. There were footrests, a pole to hold for support, a backstop, and a small wooden platform—barely as wide as the upper part of my legs—on which I sat. For security there was a seatbelt. The beauty all around magnified geometrically as we climbed. What did the Swiss think of this? Was it old hat for them? I was glad to be a tourist. I wanted to experience the full exhilarating brunt of the cosmos I was now thrust into. Even my little instamatic camera would capture some of this glory.

Once at the top near the peak, I studied each angle from where I stood. I was overwhelmed. This is mine, I determined. Totally mine. I could feel the words of the song from the scene in *Cabaret* I adored. The words defined me now. Tomorrow belongs to me.

Americans preferred Interlaken, the clerk had told me back at the train station in Bern, as if relating a well-kept secret about Grindelwald that only the natives knew. The sun was sinking behind the mountains as I made my way back to the youth hostel inside the village. I wondered if Interlaken was where I should spend the night, even believing that I was now in the most special place of all. Lunch tomorrow in Interlaken would have to make do, I decided. I could not make myself leave the Shangri-la I was now a part of.

The skies over our valley that night were merciless, with more brilliant and voluptuous stars than even at the beaches of Cyprus or at the waterfall. These Grindelwald skies were shared in my heart with Michaela, and their glory now taunted my loneliness inside. I knew this would happen. I knew I would ache for her on such a night. This most starry, starry night of all.

Chapter 18

"You're back, Nathan," Michaela welcomed with a smile as she let me into her apartment.

I gave a quick nod and walked past her into the living room.

"Hello," she said with a chuckle as she followed me. "No greeting? How was it? Did you see much? Three weeks isn't long to see Europe. Would you like a coffee?"

I sat down on her couch as I laid my backpack on the floor next to me.

"Hey, Nathan, what's up? Speak to me."

"I had a great time," I finally said while looking straight ahead.

"So tell me about it. I got a lot of studying done. And I've been excited about going to Texas. So let me tell you about that after you tell me of your adventures."

"It was a test. About us. I knew that. It was as much about me traveling around alone as about me wanting to see something of Europe."

"A test, he says. Of course, it was a test, but so what? Life is a test. Did you see much? Did you enjoy? Were there any problems? Hey, you. Lay it on me, baby."

I decided I owed her a smile. But an unconvincing half-smile is all that I managed.

"You are a pathetic creature, Nathan."

I was glad she was philosophical about my stoicism.

"I love you, Michaela," I said like a confession.

She reached over to rub my cheek.

"This guy is pathetic."

"I love Europe," I began. "I missed you, but I expected that. I wanted to see how much. I carried you around inside of me."

"Okay, that sounds promising. I feel secure in your love. I want us to be able to have a life since we will be apart so much. So. What all did you see and what was your favorite place?"

"Switzerland just blew me away," I replied. "Everything about it. The cities, the countryside, the mountains, and lakes. The farms along the way. Just perfect. I don't know how they do it, but it's as close to Heaven on earth as mankind is going to get. When I saw the Bernese Alps and places like Grindelwald and Interlaken, even Zermatt in the south, I didn't want to leave. And that's when I missed you the most. Switzerland was the first place I saw after leaving you here anyway. So there was all this love momentum about you when I entered. But it was just so perfect a place. Except it was so expensive. My God."

"Yes, it is. Even for us Germans. We want to go somewhere exotic. Exotic for us anyway. Switzerland is too close to home. But also it is even more expensive than here. Such a small country and so prosperous. And there are so many mountains there. Big mountains, I mean. You can't live or farm much in these mountains. Around them, perhaps, but that leaves a lot of land not livable for most people. So all of this makes Switzerland very demanding and expensive. We Germans want the ocean also when we vacation. We have one up by Hamburg, but Germans tend to flock to Italy and Spain, or southern France. The Mediterranean. Yugoslavia even. Like I mentioned before when you and I traveled together. Perhaps a weekend in Switzerland is good now and then, but for real vacationing, is that a word, vacationing? We want the Mediterranean."

"I saw a bit of the Mediterranean too, just now. But since we went there quite often when we were in Israel, that wasn't a major objective for me. I love history and wanted to see the historical places. But all on my stupid Eurorail. So much to do and so little time to do it and all this traveling on a free, quote unquote, train for me. First class, no less, where I can sleep comfortably, even. Not even sleep in a bed and breakfast in a town."

"Did you ever get off this train, Nathan? You did in Switzerland, you said."

"Not so much. God, I'm pathetic."

"You're an American."

"Yeah, that may explain it, but it is still pathetic. I spent the night in Grindelwald, where I first saw the Alps up close in Switzerland. They were so brilliant and beautiful and calling out to me. I much preferred Grindelwald to Interlaken. Americans love Interlaken, the word is. And yes, I see why. Me too. But Grindelwald was smack dab in the mountains. Oh, God, I think that is my favorite place in the world."

"Unless you are in a blizzard there, Nathan. Nothing is free. You can't just have a primordial paradise and get away with it. When I was a little girl, I forget how old, maybe ten, our family went to Grindelwald for a holiday. It was Christmastime, and there was a blizzard that hit just after we arrived. I don't know if you know the name for nightmare in German, but it makes perfect sense if you ever experience a blizzard in the Alps in

Grindelwald. The wind was howling. I mean howling like evil wolves trying to get at you. It was dark, freezing, and with terror winds shrieking. So somewhere in the ages of time, the word for nightmare in German became *Alptraum*. That means Alpen dream. That sounds so innocent unless you have experienced these storms. So sorry, I didn't mean to interrupt. I want to hear about your travels."

"I like the interaction with you, Michaela. Like now. Real sharing of each other so easily. So, when I saw the stars shining so brightly my one night in Grindelwald, it killed me. That's when I really, *really* missed you. Our starry, starry nights. This one without you for the first time. I missed you anyway, the entire time, but Grindelwald, in the valley, with the snow-capped mountains hovering, then these stars taunting, and me wondering where you were. Horrible. The other times without you were just longings. My night in Grindelwald without you killed me."

"I'm glad you spent the night in Grindelwald. That you weren't in such a hurry but could let yourself enjoy this paradise place."

"Yeah, I'm glad I chose to spend the night there. But it cost me time. I had to hurry even more to see other places I wanted to see. I passed right through Interlaken. So gorgeous. I understand why Americans love it. This small, quaint town right between two large and gorgeous lakes in the middle of the Bernese Alps. I wanted so badly to spend the night there also. But with no money, no time, and a free bed, so to speak, on a first-class train, I only had lunch in Interlaken and left. I did walk around, but I didn't even take a tour bus. It was that way the rest of Switzerland too. Wonderful scenery from my train through the Alps and on down to Zermatt where the Matterhorn is. Americans also love the Matterhorn. Oh, God, Zermatt was gorgeous. The ride to it alone was wonderful. Another valley to pass through. Then the town of Zermatt was wonderful, challenging Grindelwald. I had already spent a night in Switzerland, so I forced myself to settle for these train rides in and out of Zermatt. A meal, a walk around taking pictures with my little camera. That was it. Worst experience of my life was how I loved Zermatt and had to leave after only an afternoon there. Not counting the train ride in and out from Brig. I assume you know the Swiss town Brig there at the edge of that valley. Saas Fe is in that valley."

"Yes, Nathan. I know these places. Yes, very wonderful memories for me also. I'm glad I've seen them so I can relate to what you are saying without you having to explain."

"I would love to live in Zermatt as a town. It was like Christmas. I think if Christmas was a village, it would be Zermatt."

"Oh, Nathan," she said with a giggle. "You are an incurable romantic. That should go on a postcard. Maybe it is on a postcard. Did you read that while you were there? If Christmas was a village, it would be Zermatt. That's great, Nathan. Very poetic."

"Well, that's me, Michaela. Poetic and pathetically a romantic."

"*Genau*. And why I fell in love with you. Irresistible. Ha. Keep with your travels now, Nathan. I love all this."

"My memories are still forming. I'm not sure what all I saw somehow. Some is easy. The canals of Venice, the colosseum in Rome, the Eiffel Tower in Paris, all those places on postage stamps. Things you want to see and talk about for the rest of your life."

"So good, Nathan, you did see all this. We talked about it before you left. I told you some trivial things also but I wasn't sure if you would remember. Places like Montpelier in France, or Uvez. Both on the Mediterranean. It's not just the scenery but the flavor of life there. So casual, so much energy. Happiness is so easy there. I wasn't sure if you would remember any of them or if you would care the way I do. So I am glad you saw the tourist spots because they are wonderful places. Historical and charming too. And with their own lifeforce. It is easy to underrate them because they are the typical things a tourist sees. You had barely over two weeks to zoom through our portion of Europe. Rush, rush, rush. We criticize Americans for this kind of tourist travel, but I encouraged it of you. So little time and money."

"Boy, rush is the right word. It was fun except that it was horrible. Yeah, I had barely over two weeks to use that Eurorail with so little money. And I need to get back home soon. But first I must get back to my sweetheart."

"I'm not your sweetheart, Nathan. Your *Schatz*. Remember?"

"Yes, for sure, *Meine Schatz*."

"Hey, very good. You put in the feminine form of *mein* to say I am female. You should stay longer and learn German."

"Languages frustrate me. I don't know how Europeans know so many languages. I know, all these countries crammed together makes you learn them. But I grew up on the border with Mexico and in a part of Texas that speaks as much or more Spanish than they do

English, and I don't know much Spanish."

"Island America," she chided. "You can't see past yourselves. Anyway, it sounds like you didn't make it to Scandinavia."

"I kind of stuck my head in just to say I've been there. Copenhagen in Denmark for a night. One of the few places I stayed in a hostel. I slept almost always on the train. No money and no time. I passed through Stockholm in Sweden. Bought breakfast there and read an American newspaper. Then rushed to see a fjord in Norway. Man, I got to Oslo at eleven at night and it was still twilight."

"Listen, *Schatz*. Someday we will drive around much of Europe and really see these places and others you never heard of. I hate American tourists myself, but this is some karma catching up with me because I wanted you to do what you did. To go back home and know there is a Europe out there. Just a small flavor. Perhaps I will be more sympathetic to these crazy American tourists now when I go to Paris or wherever. I doubt it. But I know you are coming back here someday and we will see the real Europe together."

"You know that, do you? And how, *Meine Schatz*, do you know this? That I'll be back."

"Listen to him. Because I know it. That's how I know. It is to know. So shut up."

She walked over to sit on my lap, then planted a huge kiss on my lips. I was sure indeed that I was coming back to Europe someday.

"Where was your favorite place, Nathan? Is that a fair question? Each place is special in its own way. And each has its own experiences for you too. But is there a favorite for you?"

"Yes, for sure, I have one."

I hesitated for effect. She chuckled and kissed me again on the lips.

"So tell me, darling. You are my darling now, not my *Schatz*. We are evolving, no?"

"Jerusalem," I answered. "I loved all these places in Europe that I saw. Adored them. But every time I saw something new, I automatically compared it with Jerusalem. Jerusalem even more than the waterfall or beaches in Cyprus. Nothing in my life made a bigger impression on me than Jerusalem. The first time I saw Jerusalem with you. It's not in Europe, but still."

"Oh, yes, Nathan. Jerusalem was wonderful. I had never seen it before either. And we saw it together. How fitting. We were hitchhiking after we left the kibbutz."

"Yes. And this military truck stopped to pick us up."

"With the soldiers," she reminisced.

"Yeah. Like cattle. And they stopped for these two hitchhikers, you and me, and let us sit packed in the back of a truck to Jerusalem. And then as we approached Jerusalem, one of the soldiers got our attention and pointed."

"Oh, yes, Nathan. I got shivers. I am not religious, but I got shivers. Every drop of Jewish blood in me got shivers. I was speechless. We came in from the Mount of Olives. We had not reached the Mount of Olives yet, really, but you could see the Muslims' golden Dome of the Rock on Temple Mount of the Old City of Jerusalem. Such a tremendous energy ran through me when I saw this. The walls of the city! Then the golden onion-bulbed roof of the Russian Orthodox church on the Mount of Olives that held the convent for their nuns. All these things we could see as we drove into the Old City. All this history and significance. Yes, Nathan, that was my favorite memory as a tourist in my life, I think. I am glad you said this even though we were talking about Europe originally. And we saw Jerusalem together. You and me. Unsure about our Jewishness. But totally Jewish after our time in Israel, especially after seeing Jerusalem."

"Just stay Jewish with me, Michaela. Being a Jew is the one ethnic group or race in the world that you can convert to. You don't have to be born a Jew and you don't have to be religious. You are a Jew when you want to be one. It is treated like a race, but you can convert through the religion of Judaism. But you are Jewish when you decide to be one."

"I converted to honor my father. You were born one because of your mother. But now we are because that's what we became. By choice. This people that we are from, however it is we got here."

Chapter 19

"Our last starry, starry night together, Nathan," she said to me in a melancholy tone as we sat at an outdoor café in Freiburg. "We never made it to my mother's. That is the problem with being in a hurry. But it is best, perhaps. She may wonder why I bothered to introduce you."

"I am glad you are coming to Texas," I replied. "It makes goodbye easier. I hate sentimental farewells. Then comes the hole in your heart from the emptiness."

"Is that the word? Emptiness? Will you live through such a hardship?"

"Well, I didn't pass our first test very well. Even with all the things I did and saw while I was on the Eurorail, there was a cloud over my head. I'm a sentimental guy. Drives me crazy."

"It shows you are alive. That you have depth."

"I even like loneliness, to be honest. It just drives me crazy. I get attached to people and places easily. But loneliness makes me feel alive. Not an empty life at all, like you hear. Time for reflection. To be in tune with yourself. But living with longing."

"So this place where you will stay in Texas, it is near the university where you go? I won't have a car. I can buy a bicycle. I don't want to depend on you for everything."

"I have a car, and yes, it is near where I go to school.

Back after World War I, the university built some wooden cottages. Like you mentioned about yours here. These wooden cottages near the university were for our returning veterans. Many got married when they came home from the war. Almost the entire student body until World War I lived on campus, well within walking distance to classes and dining facilities. There were a few shops and restaurants just off campus also. In those days, not many had cars. No one had money. Even if you got married there was nowhere to go and no money to do anything anyway. I love that. That is the Texas I love. Not for being poor, but for being self-reliant. Few jobs, little money, but you made do. Even now these cottages are in good shape for their age and are cheap. We'll be cozy and snug."

"Living on love," she said with a laugh.

"Yeah. I like that. Texas at its best. The necessities and each other. Perfect."

"You make me look forward to this."

"We have a break in the middle of our semester in the spring," I said.

"I will arrive just before Christmas. I will need this Christmas pause to get my bearings. Maybe we can do something in the spring with the time off then. See some of your Texas."

"Yes, good. Everything will be set up for you. I'll be studying, and you'll need to get your bearings. Then Christmas break we can travel around a bit. We won't have to wait until spring. I want to show you some of Texas soon after you arrive."

"I want to see other parts of America too, if that's possible."

"We can do that at Christmas break, maybe. Go

outside Texas. I don't know. We'll see. Then you'll be starting spring semester with me, and we have a pause in the middle of it, like I said. Spring break, we call it. And we can go around parts of Texas. Or wherever. Even with my car we can't go too far. We only have a week off."

"It will be just like here," she moaned. "No money and no time."

"We're seasoned veterans of this kind of life. We've got it down. We'll do fine."

"I suppose. It is a challenge, but I've never been to America before. It will be such a tease to be there and be so limited in what to do."

"Then what?" I mused aloud. "What will you do after Texas? And you're only staying a semester with me? You mentioned Africa."

"Who knows what will happen? I need to graduate next year, and yes, then I want to go to Africa. Those have been my plans since before I met you. If I find a job like being a teacher in Germany, when I graduate, I may feel stuck. As if I am breaking some career plan if I leave it."

"What about us?" I asked. "Am I not in your future? It's starting to matter to me. I still don't want to get in your way and don't know what to do with my life. But you matter to me."

"I am still living one day at a time, Nathan. Just like you are doing. Plans cloud it up. We have strong feelings for one another. Our first test away from each other didn't change our longing. Soon we separate again. Then we will see how things are in Texas. That's the best I can do."

I stared off to the side in thought.

Chapter 20

I loved being a student again. I never pictured I would work on a master's degree, but here I was and taking a subject I never thought I would like. Economics. It was my history professor who talked me into this endeavor. She thought I should spread my wings in my academic life.

I always thought my college profs should do this, spread their academic wings more. Here were all these universities with all kinds of curricula and research outlets available in them, and no one cared. No one seemed to talk to anyone in another field. Renowned scientists did award-winning research, political leaders came and gave speeches, businesses gave grants, but no one seemed to speak to anyone else in this vast universe of a university. Each stayed glued to their discipline and that was the extent of their world. The profs did their job and went home to their spouse and kids or did more research. All in a day's work.

So here now was this broad world in front of me that I was part of again. Physics, engineering, social studies, liberal arts, business, laboratories, libraries. All a part of student life.

My parents were sure I was returning to college because I didn't want to settle down. That was part of it. I didn't. The rat race still seemed congested to me. And once sedentary life sucked you in, you were stuck. I had just come from worlds I'd only read about before, or had seen on the news or in some movie. Adventures in places I did not know existed.

Until I traveled.

Settling down with some mundane job, stuck in a structured setting for very long, scared the daylights out of me. I wanted more of my experiences. I loved the Marines, then traveling. I also loved the experience of the books I studied when I got my undergraduate degree. Mind-expanding and soul-searching, all of it.

Classrooms got a bad rap, as far as I was concerned. There were real life simulations or textbook analysis, and all opened me up. If books were all I knew of life, the critiques from the supposed streetwise might have merit. But mostly, these critics of academic life were dull people who were stuck knowing only narrow environments I wanted little to do with.

That was another thing I liked about Michaela. She loved adventure, travel, different cultures, and intermingling with people. And wonderfully, she loved books too. They added to the mystique of life for her. New channels and horizons. Now suddenly we would be students together. We had shared adventures and romance, and now that brought us together to my very own university.

She would be an Aggie, but I wasn't going to tell her that. There might occur some immune-suppressive disorder of her cultural DNA to anything Texan. So, I decided it best she live the day-by-day with me at Aggieland and adjust to it without knowing what was happening.

I missed her, but football season helped me out with some of that, keeping my attention, filling my time. And

I studied each day in my familiar environment without agonizing over lost symmetry with my soulmate. Each day absorbed in my studies was one day closer to home. Our home together in my abode in College Station, Texas.

We promised not to call one another. We barely had money to live on, and overseas calls were outrageously expensive. Letters took over a week to arrive. I never was sure which letter of mine she was answering. She would arrive soon, and we felt secure in that future, whatever it proved to be. A reassuring letter every few days until then was plenty to keep the heart fulfilled.

I was happy, even chirpy, in my student routine. One day led to another. I loved my courses. Economics didn't care about your religion, social class, political philosophy, or your taste in music and fashion. It told you how the world works and doesn't work when you interact with economic and monetary forces. Defy the economy and marketplace at your own risk. It didn't have anything against you. You could also jump off a cliff and pretend it wouldn't break your neck. You could print money to solve world hunger. Or redistribute wealth. It was all up to you and the implementation. It worked or it didn't. In economics class, we studied how and why the marketplace reacted to different stimuli or obstacles. I so resented politicians as I studied, and ideologues. Those who felt they had the inside edge on not only prosperity but a moral world order. Just give them the power and move out of the way.

One day I got the letter I wanted. I studied her handwriting each time to see what mood she might be in. This one was written in big bold and flowing cursive letters. She was wrapping things up in Freiburg to be on her way.

I can't believe the term is finally coming to an end, her letter began. *It doesn't seem that long ago that you left for Texas, though long enough. But now we reach our soon-to-be world. Yet another stage of our relationship. I study hard and enjoy my courses. There are no temptations from the elements to forget about you or my coming to Texas. I am on my way, my darling. My SCHATZ! I fly from Frankfurt in a week. That will give me plenty of time before Christmas to adjust. You will have Christmas break just after I arrive. I can recover from jet lag while you study for your finals. I remember talking about this before and now it is finally here. Then we can see some of Texas. I hope other places also. I am so excited, Nathan. Now the missing you is beginning to hit me hard. I can smell you. We are going to be together once again. I knew this would occur, but I was numb to it. For survival. Now I want you. I am on my way. I love you, Nathan. We are almost together.*

Chapter 21

"Hello, is this Nathan?"

It was a girl's voice on the phone, Texas accent.

"Yes, sure. Who is this, please?"

"I am in your Statistics class. I doubt you know me. I sit at the back and am very quiet. Unlike you, ha. I remember you because you made a B on a test once and challenged the prof about it. I loved that. You hate B's. Anyway, I have someone here that knows you and is looking for you. I couldn't believe it. Speaking of statistics, what's the odds of that happening? I was walking on campus between classes, and this girl walked up to me and asked about you. She's from Germany, she said, and was supposed to stay with you here and go to school. Can you believe I knew you? She just walked up to me and asked about you and I knew you. Can't get over it. Just a moment. Here she is."

"Nathan, hello, *Mein Schatz*. It's me. I have arrived. I flew into Houston this morning. It took me all day to get here. I am so exhausted. I barely slept on the plane and even less on the bus to College Station. I am on the Texas A&M campus."

"Michaela," I said excitedly. "You're here! I wasn't sure of the day exactly you would arrive. You didn't say. I even wondered why not. I could have met you at the airport. Where are you on campus now? I could have picked you up at the bus station here."

There was silence.

"Where are we please?" I heard her say distantly on the phone.

I could vaguely hear the other girl mumble something.

"Oh, yes," Michaela's voice said to the girl. "Okay. I will tell him this. Thank you."

"This girl that helped me find you told me I am at the phones area of the Memorial Student Center. She said you would know this place."

"Yes, for sure. Our student building, so to speak. Our campus living room, I guess you would say. I know where all those phones for the students to use are. Just stay there. I'm on my way. I live just off campus. We will have to hurry when I arrive. I can't show you anything. I'll park out front illegally, but it will be okay if we dash in and out."

"I'm waiting, *Schatz*. I am excited."

"You better be."

She was here, I thought joyfully as I dashed out of my cottage to my car. The full realization hit me as I drove. She really was here. Just as planned. She was back in my life!

The Memorial Student Center, or MSC as we called it, was a short distance from my house. It was just across the street from our football stadium. There was plenty of room to park, but I went to the driving enclosure in front of the MSC, for expedience. If she was waiting on me where she said, my illegal parking would be a minor problem.

Just inside the doors was the counter with the receptionist. The MSC had hotel rooms for any visitors that wanted to spend the night directly on campus. Just past the receptionist were the many phones where students or visitors could make local calls. This is where Michaela was to be. I searched the many figures in the area.

There she was. And looking at me. I wanted to get dramatic like in a movie, but it would have taken something away from the moment. No drama needed. Just to see her again.

"You found me," she chirped, looking up at me from our hug.

"We've got to go, though," I replied. "I'm parked illegally. They have buses that drive this little inlet here in front. I left room for any bus to pass my car, but just in case, we need to hurry. Where are your things?"

"Just here," she said pointing back toward the reception counter. "Only my backpack. There by the couch in front of us."

"That's it?" I asked. "You're here half a year or however much, and that's it?"

"Don't act so surprised, my dear. That's how we both traveled around Israel and Europe, if you remember."

"Yeah, but that's when we were bumming around. We're living here now."

"If I need anything, I can buy it here. These are my essentials. Even a nice dress is in that small rucksack. Jeans, underwear, a dress, a couple of blouses and three T-shirts. I want to buy some American things, Texas things, Texas A&M things. So."

"Okay. Let me be a gentleman and carry your backpack to the car."

"I will absolutely let you. I am so tired, Nathan. I want to go straight to bed. We can eat first. Take me somewhere, though. I don't want to wait for you to cook, and I'm too tired to cook. I've tasted some of your cooking, too. So let's unload my things into our new love cottage and then you take me somewhere to eat. We'll talk, and then I'm crashing. Perfect word for how I feel. I feel like to crash land on your bed. Our bed, I mean. How big is our bed, by the way? Big enough, I hope. I want to be cozy with you, of course, but I want room to spread out too."

"It's an entire double bed. How's that? Not even a one-and-a-half. A full double bed. It's really only a mattress. I don't have a bed frame. Just a mattress on the floor."

"Perfect. Easier to collapse and crash, then."

The thrill of having her back in my life overwhelmed me. I felt like strutting as I walked to the car.

"Such a spacious campus," she said as we drove past the basketball gym toward the south end of the campus. "A stadium, a basketball house, and right across the street an empty park. My goodness, Nathan. And I see so many buildings all around."

"Texas," I emphasized. "Texas is about the size of France."

"Such old houses," she remarked. "I thought Texans were rich."

"These houses here are for students. This town was built especially for the college a hundred years ago. It was prairie until then. The professors and any businesses are in the next town. The next town is the county seat. Where the *Burgermeister* would live, you might say."

We were home in just a few minutes.

"Hardly any traffic," she remarked as we drove into

my driveway. "That makes it good for riding a bicycle to class."

"That's what most of the students do. Ride their bicycles. Most have cars, but mostly for shopping or going out. The normal daily life is to ride your bike to class, then around campus if you need, then back home. Stores are around, restaurants, and a few bars. That's about it. A drab college town. Perfect for studying. Just enough extracurricular to keep from going crazy and then back to studying."

"Is everyone so smart then?" she asked.

"It's not the Harvard of Texas, like Freiburg was back at your home, but it probably has as many good students. It is a state-supported school, the oldest in Texas, and lets in some not as smart as well. Smart enough, but not special. Just trying to educate its populace. Mostly engineers and farmers, but a strong Liberal Arts college too. It has the best and brightest, but some students are only just above normal."

"Liberal Arts, you say. Good, that's what I will be studying. I will be taking only three courses. I am here mostly for my English. But I arranged that I can audit some courses here. History, both American and Texas. I don't have to take tests. But I must write a thesis paper for each class when I return to get my credit. Credit just for English, not the history I learned. So I must study as if a student, just not as meticulously in such detail. I am looking forward to this."

I pulled into our driveway.

"We're here," I said. "This is our love nest for the next few months."

She looked at me just before opening the door to get out of the car.

145

"And I look forward to us," she said with a gleam.

"Welcome, Michaela. Finals are near, and I can't take you around much. But you will love it here. This will be our Texas version of the same old thing."

"Sounds marvelous, my dear."

I grabbed her backpack from the rear seat and led her into the house.

"This is the living room," I explained as we entered. "I study in here. It's attached to the dining room, as you see. I use the table to eat and to study. A refrigerator, gas stove, two chairs."

"A television," she said.

"It's small. I don't watch much. I study until about two every night, even on weekends. Every once in a while I watch the news or a little football. That's it. You're welcome to use it. I won't challenge your choices much."

"I will watch a bit. I don't have to study so much, and in a way television is part of the study. I've seen some American shows, though. Very silly. I want to say stupid."

"You can say stupid. That's a good description. So I wouldn't watch too much anyway."

We walked on into the bedroom.

"The toilet is attached to the bedroom," she remarked. "That doesn't bother you?"

"It hasn't until now. The shower is in there too. It's convenient, in fact."

"I suppose."

"And here is our mattress on the floor."

"Ah, Nathan, very nice. Perfect size. It's so long. Yes, you are tall. It takes half the room. No wonder you study in the dining room."

She walked to the wall on the far end, by the window.

"A guitar. Good. I want to hear you play, Nathan."

"No, you don't. I'm teaching myself. I'm lousy. I know three progressions, one of them a minor one—just simple chords. To unwind. Plus, I write music."

"You do? That is wonderful. You must sing me one of your songs, then. I love this, Nathan. You are so full of life."

"I wrote a song in high school. I still remember it. I wanted to see if I could do it. All these Country singers I grew up hearing, so many of them wrote about their lives. That intrigued me. I write stories, too, a bit. I want to be a writer. And music moves me, too. And then there was the Beatles. They wrote their own songs. And guys like Buddy Holly. He's from Texas. It just made me want to do it. So I dabble."

"I came to the right place. Yes. This will be a marvelous experience. More than just to see a new place and learn my courses. New life aspects also. I am really looking forward to this. New horizons here."

"And new foods. You're starving. We have some German dishes in the next town, the county seat I was telling you about. I'm not sure where, though. Since you're so hungry, you may want to try your own cuisine. But I would have to find out where these German restaurants are. Texas had a lot of German immigrants in its past. Lucky for you. You can eat well because of it."

"Never mind. Everyone eats American food too. Fast food."

"Do you like Mexican? Have you tried it? It and barbecue are the popular meals in Texas. A lot of restaurants have these. And we have fast food, since you brought it up. Meaning dishes so popular the restaurants just shovel it out. Always some on the fire for eager customers."

"Fast food doesn't sound so appetizing. But I am hungry."

"It's up to you."

"Wherever. Just take me somewhere."

I pointed out restaurants along the way and described the food they served. But I knew where I wanted to take her.

"The guy that owns this restaurant used to play football for Texas A&M," I told her as we waited for our order. "He kicked the longest field goal in Southwest Conference history at the time. Now he owns a restaurant specializing in barbecue. Barbecue is a recipe. A special sauce. I'll order for you. It's real good."

"I don't know what you are talking about, Nathan. It is like I am in a foreign country. Ha. Barbecue. Football. And I know you don't mean soccer football. Field goal. I don't even know what else you were talking about. I guess I have to learn English after all."

"Good."

Chapter 22

"You take your studies so seriously, Nathan," Michaela praised as I drove. "You not only study until two every night, you hardly take a break. And you work out physically also. Like you did in Israel. You are impressing me even more. I am so glad school is finished for the semester. Finals are over for you now. I need a break just from taking care of you while you studied."

"Much of Texas," I said, choosing my own subject of conversation, "will bore you, I think. I mean as you look out the window, anyway. It's different enough to make you curious, but most is flat until you get out into the far western part of the state. We do have some hills in the middle. The far west part will look like the cowboy movies some. Even the people somewhat. A more modern version of a Western. Cars instead of horses. Some brick houses. Everything else like out of a movie."

"Where are we going now? These cowboy places you speak about?"

"Everywhere is cowboy, some. But I want to relax and for you not to be bored. Maybe we'll see these open spaces someday. We have almost two weeks now between semesters because of Christmas. That's enough to show you something. But it's just long open dry spaces out west, the cowboy setting I mentioned. The far west is interesting, but it gets redundant after a while. So I'm going to take you to Galveston. That's on the coast.

South of Houston. It's cold this time of year. Not as bad as in Germany, but cold like what we just left in College Station. A bit less cold than College Station. But it means we can't go swimming in the ocean. It's still nice to walk along the beaches though. It'll be cloudy a lot, but there will be some starry, starry nights for us too. There is some interesting history there. We'll spend about a week. Then we'll get focused for next semester."

The highway that ran through College Station ran all the way to Galveston. It was a Texas rural highway that passed through the western edge of Houston. I normally would have stayed outside of Houston, but I wanted to show her some of our largest metropolis. A vibrant, prosperous town where a lot of America seemed to want to live these days.

"My goodness, Nathan," Michaela said, amazed. "I didn't know Texas had such cities like we just left. No cowboys in Houston. Or I didn't see any where you drove."

"Houston has everything, including a lot of cowboys. Cowboy in culture, at least. Or doing business with cowboys. A lot of rural people are moving here. People from all over America are moving here. A thousand new families move here a month, I heard. It drives me crazy though. I'd live here rather than starve, and I like the zoo here and the planetarium and such. But it's too big and condensed for the likes of me. You get stuck on a freeway here and you may never get off. I got stuck on one and managed five miles in thirty minutes."

"Why don't they build more highways, then?"

"They are. That's all they do here is build. Gotta make room for the immigrants from the rust belt."

"What's the rust belt?"

"Some of our factories up north are not as competitive as they used to be. Factories are closing down there. So they call it the rust belt. Dead or dying. Plus, the economy overall is changing there too. Like a lot of places. More high-tech companies now and service-type businesses. More and more insurance companies and hotels and restaurants. The economy and demography are changing up north, but everywhere else too. Including here."

"Like in Germany. Like we talked. We were devastated after the war. You adapt or you die. But America is big, so many come now to Texas and California. And now here I am too. There are so many options in America."

"Everything is changing. I see it, and we're studying about it now in my classes. People don't necessarily eat more now, but spend more for food. That's because all kinds of new recipes are popping up affordably. More people want lobster now or filet mignon, not just meat loaf or chicken-fried steak. There's more jobs, bigger salaries, so people don't just eat, they dine. Even at home, they buy better quality foods already prepared. A lot of new businesses are opening up too. Different types of businesses. The economy has more depth now. And here in Houston there's the new space age boom. Used to be oil, cowboys, and a huge port in Houston. Now we're sending people to the moon, but it's more than that. Satellites are used for everything now, even to bounce signals off to get to our antennas on earth. So new industries and jobs for that. Especially in Texas and especially in Houston. And better-paying jobs that sound glamorous. So many of these displaced people from shriveling factories up north are coming down to our

modern and expanding economy in Texas. I miss the old
Texas, but all this excites me too. I don't know what to
make of it all since I'm so old-fashioned. I like country
boys and cotton fields and cattle ranches. Texas still has
a lot of that, but a lot of the new too. So Houston is the
center for so much of the old and new."

"You are such an interesting person, Nathan. You
were like this in Israel, too, when we traveled together.
You don't just live here, you are in the middle of
everything. That's what made you interesting to me. I'm
enjoying the trip with you just sitting in a car."

"We're getting close to Galveston now," I said while
ignoring her praise.

"The terrain is much different here," she remarked
while looking out the window. "The plants and shrubs
are different. Some of them anyway. The soil color and
texture is changing. As we approach the ocean, I
suppose."

I nodded in agreement with her observation.

"When I came first came to A&M," I reminisced,
"everybody harped about Galveston. The most beautiful
beach in the world or whatever. It is indeed very pretty
and the town is very nice. But I'm from Padre Island.
Somehow, only the locals back home knew about Padre
Island. If you ever heard anything about Padre Island,
they were probably talking about the Corpus Christi area.
That also is very nice and pretty. Padre Island is a
hundred and twenty miles long. An island, but a barrier
reef. Narrow, like a mile or two wide, for a hundred and
twenty miles just off the main coastline of Texas. It starts
at the Rio Grande River area where I'm from. That's
where America, in particular Texas, begins. And Mexico
is on the other side of the Rio Grande."

"Why don't we go there, then, Nathan?" she asked. "I would like to see where you live, and a better beach. But also Mexico."

"It's six hours just to drive to Mexico, Michaela. I know we have time. We'll do it at spring break. We get a week off then. I want to show you my home state, but I'm tired from studying and don't want to travel so far. I haven't been to Galveston in years. And it's winter. A bit cold for a beach. We'll enjoy Galveston the town as much as the beach. Christmas lights up and everything, too. Yeah, we'll go to my home at spring break. You'll get to compare."

"Good," she replied. "I would like to see a bit of Mexico. You've given me some ideas. I'll think about all of this and prepare our trip. When is spring break?"

"In March. Middle of March."

"Good. That gives me time and something to do while you're up all night studying."

"Padre Island ends right at the Corpus Christi area." I continued my explanation. "This barrier reef island is mostly a wildlife preserve. We humans are limited in our access to it. But the northern tip of the island and the southern one are for humans. And we frolic there. But now Padre Island is starting to catch on. More and more people are now finding out about South Padre Island where I'm from. It is helping the local economy."

"It's being commercialized, you mean. I know people need the money somehow, but now you are making me disappointed. You made it sound so pristine. Like when we were on Cyprus."

"Where we fell in love."

She looked at me nostalgically.

"Padre Island will be our second honeymoon,

Nathan. Not bad for never being married."

I nodded and gave a wink.

"Anyway, back to our coastline," I replied. "Where we're headed. Galveston. I went with my best friend to Galveston my freshman year at A&M. Way back. I was expecting better than South Padre Island, the way people talked. I was so disappointed. I missed the ocean, so it was great to be back on the beach, any beach, and it was nice for sure, but nothing compared to where I grew up. It is like the old saying, it's not what you know but who you know. If people know about Galveston and want to rave about the beach at Galveston, do it. Good luck. It keeps South Padre left alone for us. Almost unspoiled. But like I say, South Padre Island is catching on now, and they are starting to build it up. Plus, Mexico is just a few miles away as some travelers' encore. Where I grew up is the southernmost tip of the continental United States. We are so far south and remote that people still don't make it down there much. But we got 'em beat when it comes to tourist attractions. Natural ones. It's still our little secret. So, ha! Rave on about all these other places."

"You're spoiling Galveston for me now, Nathan."

"Not for long. You'll love it."

Chapter 23

"The Christmas lights are so nice," Michaela commented as we drove south on the island.

"Yes. It helps make up for not enough sun out now. Christmasy is nice. That'll work, I guess. It's still warm enough that we can walk on the beach barefoot, I think."

"Where are we going? You act like you know what you are doing."

"I reserved a hotel room for us. It had to be cheap, but not depressing and old. I asked a friend of mine from this area and he gave me a place and phone number. I usually don't come so prepared, but it's winter and the holidays, and I was told Galveston could be crowded. I didn't want to drag you here and we be stranded."

"Is the hotel near the beach?"

"The whole island is near the beach. The town hovers along the narrow interior. So the beach itself doesn't have much structure on it. A few restaurants, maybe. We can't just get out of our hotel room and walk straight onto the beach. It's across the highway. We'll walk from our hotel to the beach in a few minutes, and then stroll along."

She nodded approval.

"Galveston is a nice town," I commented as I drove. "And it is a wonderful beach almost as a part of the town. But I miss South Padre Island every time I come here. Any beach pretty much makes me miss Padre Island.

There's so many good beaches in Texas."

"What did you think of the beaches we went to in Israel and Greece? They were lovely, and we had wonderful times."

"I can't say any were better than Padre. But they were all so exotic in their own way. I almost can't compare. When I was on the Mediterranean, or on some beach in the Pacific Ocean, they were part of a new culture for me. With some rich history to go with it. Like Haifa or Eilat or on Santorini or Ios. Ibiza. Okinawa. I don't compare with all that. Each was another world."

"Our beaches in Germany are all up north. Even in the summer the water is cold. In the winter it is impossibly cold. Most of the year we are doing what you and I are doing now. Looking for a nice beach somewhere south where we can stroll if the weather allows. It is so cold most of the time in northern Europe. Often much colder than here right now, your winter. And overcast. Perhaps rain and snow. So we Europeans need our Greece and Spain. Maybe Crete or Israel if we want to adventure."

I stared at a sign on a small two-story wooden hotel.

"That's it," I remarked. "This is our hotel."

"It's cozy," she commented. "I'm so glad we didn't bring more than our rucksacks. Our old reliable rucksacks. I'm so glad I didn't get rid of mine."

The sun shone to the point of tempering the cold air. Perfect weather for any other place. But still too cold to fully enjoy the beach.

"Your room is ready for you," the hotel clerk instructed. "You can park to the side of the entrance here. Your room is just to the edge of the building."

"Thanks," I answered. "We don't have much

luggage. We can easily hand carry."

We walked to the car and grabbed our things.

"I'll leave the car here for now. After we drop our things, we'll get something to eat."

I was glad we were hungry. I wanted to drive around the island for a while before I strolled the beach. Looking for a restaurant that suited us was an excuse to do so.

"Seafood," Michaela said while pointing in front of our car. "I know there will be a lot of seafood restaurants, but this one is in big letters. Shall we? It looks like a good restaurant. Spacious and clean."

"It looks like a local restaurant. I don't recognize the name anyway. Yeah, let's eat native. Let's check it out."

There were pictures of John Wayne on the walls inside the restaurant. Apparently, he came here once. Maybe when he made the movie about the oilfields years ago. Or maybe they were just pictures of John Wayne because this is Texas.

"Marvelous meal," Michaela complimented the waitress as she presented our check to be paid. "What was it?"

"Flounder," she replied.

"But flounder is a northern fish, isn't it?" Michaela quizzed. "I hoped to have some of the local fish."

"That's what your boyfriend ordered," the waitress replied. "We don't serve local seafood anyway. There is fishing that goes on in the area, but it gets marketed in Houston or wherever for more money. We don't buy from these little local fishermen. They don't haul in enough to meet all the demand for the Houston area. We don't want to worry about that. People come here to get away. Eating seafood on the ocean makes them happy and they just assume it's local. Probably some of it is, by accident."

I let out a chuckle and shrugged my shoulders.

"She's right," I said. "I knew flounder was a northern fish. I could have gotten trout, but that's probably from Maine or wherever. I prefer flounder, but it doesn't really matter. Seafood is healthy, so let's just enjoy. It adds to the sense of getting away. So. Hey. What d'ya want?"

"Silly boy," Michaela said with a chuckle as we got up to leave. "Spoils it a bit. But it doesn't matter."

"Let's drive around some more," I said as we got back into the car.

The highway was a narrow two-lane paved road right in the middle of the narrow island. As we drove southward, we could see the mainland to our right and the Gulf of Mexico to our left. Ships and tankers were scattered over the water in the distance.

"It feels like a honeymoon," I said as I drove. "Again."

"It does, doesn't it. But it always does."

She looked at me with longing in her eyes.

"I'm happy," she said just above a whisper.

Her words touched me. As if from a deep poem. She couldn't have said anything better to move me like she just did.

"Are we going to get married someday?" I asked her.

"Don't, Nathan. I don't know. I don't want to think about it. We're in the middle of it, so let that be enough for now. I'm hoping there are answers for us someday. But right now, let's just be happy. That's perfect."

"I know. I'm not ready to settle down. But I don't know if I can ever leave you." I shook my head as I gave a sigh. "Okay, we're in the middle of us right now. I'll go with that. It just makes me feel good to talk about it sometimes anyway."

She reached over to hold my hand.

"I love you, Nathan. I have never been so in love."

Neither one of us could talk. Touching hands and looking out at the ocean absorbed us.

"So," I finally said to bring us back to earth. "Let me tell you a bit about Galveston."

"There is something to tell?" she asked. "Every place has a story, but so what? I am here for a beach holiday."

"You don't know our history," I answered. "That's the point in all of this. Not just to get away or be in love. But here you are. Even on Christmas holiday you are still here as a student. We have a marvelous history. Things besides the Alamo or cowboys and Indians."

"Okay, I am all ears. Is that what you say to show you are paying attention? I heard that anyway. So I am all ears here. Tell me about this marvelous Galveston."

"When the New World was opening to the influx of European immigrants and colonialists," I began, "Texas was part of New Spain. Spain took over most of South and Central America and several Caribbean islands. Among the very first settlers were Jews trying to escape the Inquisition. The Inquisition followed them around, though, but you could still find somewhere to escape to. The Indians in Texas were particularly fierce. Especially the Comanches. Great horsemen and savage warriors. So settlement was sparse. Something like only three thousand Europeans lived in what is now Texas by the early nineteenth century. It became something of a pirate base. The most colorful and successful was this French privateer named Jean Lafitte. He was based much of the time in the New Orleans area. He was French but spied for Spain to check out any signs of a revolt. Texas and New Spain were always restless. He ended up in Galveston."

"So one of your main early characters was a pirate?"

"There were quite a few pirates, but LaFitte is the most famous. He was a hero fighting along with Andrew Jackson in the Battle of New Orleans against the British. And he came in handy other times too, but mostly he was a nuisance. A colorful one. Galveston was an interesting place right from the beginning."

"Because of the natural ports?"

"Not just the ports. Because of the Comanche Indians in the interior and the Karankawa in the Galveston and coastal region, there were not many settlers in early Texas. That's the biggest reason these pirates liked Galveston. Great port and no governments around to bug them. They made a nice little enclave at Galveston and Indianola. Places like that. Pirates and privateers could come and go at will for a while. Loot and rob ships, then run to Galveston, a basically uninhabited foreign country."

"That is fascinating. Texas was a wild place. Fierce Indians, pirates, then cowboys."

"After Mexico rebelled against Spain, then Texas against Mexico—you heard of the Alamo probably—Texas became an independent country, then part of America. A lot of German immigration started coming through these ports. Galveston became the biggest city in Texas. Then it got wiped out by severe hurricanes. Indianola basically ceased to exist. Galveston struggled and built a seawall, which we are on now. But the city was so damaged it never really recovered. Yep, Galveston was big, wealthy, and growing until that hurricane in 1900. The most destructive natural disaster in American history. In the meantime, the main port of Texas moved from Galveston to Houston. So Houston is this huge metropolis that is thriving today, while Galveston is a nice getaway, so to speak. And look at the houses and shops. Part of the rebuilding was they elevated their houses and business structures on stilts. And by having the bottom floor be a basement or garage to take the brunt of the storms, they could survive."

"My goodness. Who would want to live here? I would love to live here except for hearing your story. Do they still get wiped out by hurricanes?"

"Not like in 1900, but it still gets some bad ones. Hurricanes are still a threat. Houston gets it bad sometimes too, but they've got drainage down better with time. It used to be swampland all around Houston. Malaria pockets, too. But they drained the swamps and it's livable. But still some hurricanes."

"Why would anyone put up with this?"

"Because it's a great place to live. You just have to know a hurricane may happen every few years, and one of those hurricanes might be horrific. They are learning how to deal with it better. Draining the swamps helped. It's still lowland, and the area floods easily. But things like the seawall help. Even though severe hurricanes don't happen so often, anytime a tropical storm starts off the coast of Africa, they have to worry. The worry eats at you."

"If it is worth it to people to stay, then okay. My goodness. I can see why they want to live here, I guess, but I don't see how it is worth it. To each his own."

"Yeah. I grew up on the coast too. Near Padre Island, like I said. We got a couple of horrific hurricanes while I was growing up. And some lesser ones. And tropical storms. Our farm was a bit inland though, and the brunt was usually manageable."

"Let's choose a beach now, Nathan. I want to feel the sand on my feet. The water running through my toes."

I chose an area that had a few cars parked on the sand.

"Oh, this is marvelous, Nathan," Michaela swooned as we walked. "It makes you want to live here. Hurricanes or not. I can see now why people risk it."

"While Galveston was being formed," I began again with my historical account, "the Karankawa Indians menaced the new settlers. These Karankawa were fierce fighters, and cannibalistic. A double whammy. And huge in stature. Up to seven feet tall. We wiped them all out. Even after they were conquered and their land taken, people would kill them just because they were Indians. No cultural heritage of theirs to share, no live and let live, nothing. And even for selfish greed they could be handy in the present work force. Imagine what kind of athletes they would be. We'd be winning national championships in football and basketball with these guys around. So even if you are imperialist and racist, just for practical reasons, find a way to manage better. Racism is a monster. And stupid too."

"You get into things, Nathan. Do you think of things like this in your spare time?"

"I like to think about stuff, yeah. I get curious easily."

"I would rather concentrate on the ocean between

my toes, if you don't mind."

"Yeah, me too," I replied. "It's depressing to think about what we did to the Karankawa."

'So let's think about the moon coming over this oceanic horizon in a few hours. With the Christmas lights around. So romantic."

"Another advantage of not being married. These honeymoons following us around."

She wrapped her arm around my waist. How was I ever going to let go of her? The thought of being independent someday didn't feel good at all.

Chapter 24

"I had a disagreement in class today with my professor," Michaela said as we sat at our table for supper. "He was correct in his facts, but he missed the point in a historical sense to me. How the Magna Carta was the beginning of Western constitutionalism and individual rights. He didn't seem to visualize the extent that it diminished war, civil war in particular. He did understand all that, but he seemed so indifferent. Europe was changing so quickly in the thirteenth century when the Magna Carta came about. There were enough wars already. Even after the Magna Carta there were so many wars and civil wars. America is a new country. You had a revolution and then a civil war. But America wanted nothing to do with Europe and avoided all the wars we were having. Until the twentieth century, anyway. I don't blame you, but I am a European. We were ravaged again and again and had to fight for any new right. So that is why his indifference—condescension is a better word— about all the struggles we've had through the centuries irritated me. I am so grateful for the Magna Carta. It is more personal to me, I suppose. I am auditing his class. I was out of place. We even agreed on principle. It just stirred me up to see how America was so superior to us in his mind. The Magna Carta helped form your thoughts and legal system, but you got to live halfway around the world and not have to deal every day with protecting yourselves from the old feudal system and the old way of thought."

"I'm sure you flashed with him. I do it a lot, but I'm not auditing any courses."

"I will behave myself. I like it here and studying here. I don't need to make problems."

"Well, I love you being here. I love being a student here too, and it is perfect I'm sharing it all with you."

"Cozy, isn't it?"

I nodded with a smile.

"I almost hate going back, Nathan. I miss home and want to go back. Trouble is, I am so snug here. I don't want it to end. How much of this are we going to take? This is always happening to us."

"It's a few months away, still. We don't have to worry about it yet."

"But it's my happiness here with you that makes me worry about it. I can live in denial about it for a while. But another goodbye will be at hand someday. Someday soon."

I looked away and blew out a huff.

"You don't want to talk about it," she said. "I don't either. I am sorry I brought it up."

I kept my stare away from her while letting my frustration show.

"I'm not ready to settle down either," I replied.

"Life is supposed to be complicated. It certainly is with us."

I got up and walked to the other side of the room. I picked up my guitar and brought it back to the desk. I pulled the chair farther out to give me room to strum.

"I wrote this song," I said while looking up at her.

"You've written several songs since I've been here.

None about me."

"Well, I have now. Written a song about you."
A broad smile gushed onto her face.
"And you're going to sing it for me now?"
"Yep."
I strummed more on the guitar.
"It's in A minor. My favorite progression. Perfect."
I hummed some of the melody to fit it to the chords.
"To you, my dear," I said with a wink.
"See that tree standing over there
Can't you hear it singing with the wind
Leaves get blown so quickly
Scattered everywhere.

Yes, there's thousands of these leaves
And their paths are one with wind and sky
But there's one leaf especially
That always makes me think
My thoughts of you.

It keeps on flying
Farther, farther
Searching for its luck
The things it sees
All make it hard
To go back home.

It's always meeting other leaves
That it finds from near and distant trees
Then with one or another
It drifts away in peace
One with the wind.

The leaf goes farther

Always farther
Never to return
Until it knows
It's found its way
To destiny.

It so often happens
While the wind seeks out its destiny
There is left a yearning
To never lose its faith
In love again."

I looked up from the guitar for her reaction. She seemed fighting a smile, then ruffled her hair playfully with her hands.

"I love it, Nathan. I was sure I would need to pretend to like it and somehow convince you that I did. But I love it. The melody is happy and flowing. And the words don't rhyme. Somehow it is deeper for it. The words are about you as much as me, but they are to me, and I love them. I will take them. Cherish them. No one has ever written a song about me before. God! I have my own Wolfgang Amadeus Mozart."

"Me and Wolfgang you're saying? I'll grab that."

"What kind of song will you write about me if we don't make it?"

"I'm sure we'll never know," I replied.

Chapter 25

"So, Nathan, when are you going to show me your Padre Island? Should we go there first for spring break? Are we going to have enough time for the beach if we go to Mexico?"

"We should go to Mexico first," I mused. "Are you getting excited to travel again? Spring break is not until next week. I usually stay put on my spring breaks, to study."

"Oh, what a horrible idea, Nathan. But you were in Israel last spring. So what are you talking about?"

"Yes, but while I finished up my bachelor's degree here, before that, I studied during that week of spring break. In my early years I didn't. I didn't take studying as seriously when I first became a college student. I was just out of high school and freedom excited me. We didn't have a spring break back then anyway. Only Easter break, which was half the time off as now. But when I came back to finish my bachelor's, after the Marines, I was studious. I was very serious by then, and I stayed put for all holidays to study."

"I admire that, I suppose. You're giving me a bad conscience. Like I'm dragging you away. I so want to see Mexico and your Padre Island. I leave back for Germany in two months."

"I want to see these places with you. We only have a week. We can't go too far into Mexico. I grew up by the border and never made it farther than Monterrey. So I would like to see these places myself. Mexico has pyramids down south, by Mexico City. And just west of those are the ruins at Oaxaca. I'm intrigued by them. The ruins at Oaxaca and the pyramids near Mexico City are from hundreds of years ago. From when Mesoamerican tribes ruled. Everyone's heard of the Mayans. They invented the concept of zero and were first rate astronomers."

"The Hindu in India invented zero," she corrected.

"They both did, independently," I corrected back. "Halfway around the world from each other and at about the same time. It's like something was going on in the world back then. Some cosmic vibration or something."

"Sort of like just before the time of Jesus," she added. "There was Zoroaster, then Judaism, then Christianity, but off in India and China at the same approximate time, was Hinduism and Buddhism. Each distinct, but so much of the same spiritual fabric. Like waves of a new spirit flowing through the air or something."

"No one knows where these pre-Mayan Indians came from," I said to follow through on our original thoughts. "I mean there are certain archaeological records and myths from back then in the Americas. But so much is not known. So many mysteries. Here are all these new concepts worldwide going on, within just a few hundred years of each other. Even halfway around the world from each other and independent of each other. So we have to wonder, was there a space alien colony behind all this, or some mode of travel we aren't aware of that passed it to the four corners of the earth?"

"I love being a student, Nathan. I could do this the

rest of my life. Just study life. And wonder in awe about all these events and places."

"Part of the study of life is to live it."

"Exactly, but also I have regrets that we end up so tied down. It seems to limit curiosity after a while. I know not completely, but when you are a student, so many new worlds and disciplines are delivered to us on silver platters. So I know we must settle down. I even want to someday, but I have regrets about it also, like now, just thinking about the pyramids in Mexico. Or Egypt. Who wants to settle down with all this available to us?"

"Yeah," I concurred. "I love this stuff too. So, more important than Padre Island are these ruins. We'll ride the bus to Oaxaca and look out the window while we go there. We'll intermingle with passengers along the way, and eat the local cuisine. But the key to the whole adventure now is these ruins in Oaxaca and Mexico City."

"I want to go to San Luis Potosi also. It is up in the north of Mexico. I think a couple of hours inside the border. Why can't we take your car there? Why are we taking a bus?"

"Because they'll steal my American car or break into it. And you have to worry about cops giving you a ticket, or with being insured, even if you didn't do anything wrong. We're at the whim of some cop if he's in the mood to go after us. It's a hassle for Americans. Otherwise, I'd love to take my car. We'll take it to McAllen. That's where I grew up. Near there. My sister and her husband live there. It's right on the border. We'll leave my car at their place, and they can take us to the bus station at the border. San Luis Potosi is almost due south of McAllen. There will be a bus to take us there. I've never been there. What attracts you about it?"

"It has an artist village. A special one. It will give me a feel for Mexico. A good one. Besides getting on a bus and staring out the window for hours."

"Sounds good. I'm game. I've read up on San Luis Potosi. For a couple or so years it was the capital of Mexico. Mexico for a few years was a French colony. Back about the time we were fighting our Civil War here in America. And with all the turmoil against the French, the rebellious Mexicans caused enough problems that the non-French capital was San Luis Potosi. And it was a Texas-born Mexican general who defeated the French in Puebla, Mexico, which pretty much secured a successful rebellion against the French. He was from Goliad, this Texas-born Mexican general. Goliad is famous in Texas history. Right after the Alamo, the Mexican army moved on to take the rest of Texas. In Goliad, which isn't all that far from Galveston, the Mexican army won another victory against an outnumbered Texas army. Like with the Alamo, all the Texans were slaughtered. So the cry rang out from that point on, 'Remember the Alamo, Remember Goliad.' Well, little old Goliad produced the general that later defeated the French in Puebla."

"Nathan, I know you love history and all, and you're very interesting, and I am here to learn about Texas and America, but how did we get from traveling by bus to San Luis Potosi on our first day of spring break, to defeating the French for independence almost a hundred years before you or I were ever born?"

"Well, Michaela darling, you wanted to go to San Luis Potosi. Lo and behold, this famous general that defeated the French was from Texas, and because of his defeating the French, the capital was moved to San Luis Potosi. What's your problem? I love knowing this, and if you love me, you will open up to me and this history I'm talking about."

"He is holding me hostage with love as the ransom. Women are supposed to do that to men. You are like this saying I heard. If I ask you the time, Nathan, please don't tell me how to build a clock. Isn't that a saying here in America? I think whoever made such a statement must have known you."

"I love history, Michaela. And I love you."

"That explains things, I am sure. I am grateful you love me. And I am sure from all this that it is a sign I will know all about Mexico by the time we return to finish the semester."

Chapter 26

"Why didn't you bring your passport, Nathan?"

"Because I'm American and they want our tourist dollars. They make it easy for us to be a tourist."

"Except that I needed mine just now."

"You are German. You could have pretended you were American, but if they had any questions at all and found out you were German, then that would be a problem for you. And you don't want problems here. You don't want them in America either, but I guarantee you don't want to make problems here."

"Yes, I have been to many third-world countries. Even Spain as part of the EU can be too complicated for me sometimes. But now that we are on the bus to San Luis Potosi, let me give you my money belt. It has my passport and traveler's checks."

She discreetly passed her money belt to me, then casually returned to looking out the window of the bus.

"It is so dry here," she commented. "Arid is the word in English. I wanted to see the Texas landscape of the movies. But we went to Galveston instead. Now here we are. I am seeing these cactus plants and desert, or at least semi-desert. Watch what you ask for."

She returned to her travel guide, then looked at me with emphasis from what she had just read.

"Six thousand feet," she commented. "That's how high we will be when we arrive in San Luis Potosi."

"It's part of the Rocky Mountain chain. I doubt it says that in your book, but whatever chain it is called, it is part of the vast scheme of the Rockies. Like in El Paso they have the Davis Mountains and all, but as part of the broader chain of the Rocky Mountains."

"Oh, my God, Nathan, there are one and a half million people in San Luis Potosi. We are on a bus. How will we get around? I don't know what to see, really. A market. The artist colony—I want to see that. We don't have so much time. We'll see that and continue on from there to Oaxaca today somehow."

"Man, this ride is forever," I whined. "I thought it was just a couple of hours. That was Monterrey on my mind, I guess. It's pretty here, but I want to be there."

"Like a child, Nathan. Be patient. Perhaps we'll find a hotel to spend the night after all. Oaxaca is the same distance from San Luis Potosi as McAllen is. Looking at the map it seems that to me. Be patient. It's on the way. We don't have to sidetrack to see my artist village."

"We're not spending the night, Michaela. We'll find your artist colony and then get the hell out of there. I want to see Oaxaca and the pyramids. We focus on that."

She looked at me to mock a military salute, then returned to the landscape out the window.

We arrived in the early afternoon. Enough time to find the artist village. Except...how do you find an artist village in a metropolis on foot?

"Take a taxi," the lady at the information counter suggested. "This is Mexico. It is cheap. Too many bus connections. Take a taxi."

"Taxis are cheap, but when you are a gringo, you have to hassle," I complained to the lady. "The locals assume you are rich. Even if you are a college student living on nothing."

The lady looked unfazed at my disgruntlement. I psyched myself for the confrontations that were waiting outside.

"Too much," I argued back with the taxi driver.

"Not too much. You are American. I have big family. Gas is expensive. I have expensive car. Not too much."

"Gas isn't expensive in Mexico," I sneered. "I'm not going to pay your fare."

"Where you get a taxi?" he sneered back.

"Almost anywhere besides you."

"Okay, get in. I take you to artist village. Many Americans. They pay good money. Not you. You cheapskate American."

I looked at Michaela.

"That's good information," I told her. "Remember that when we talk to the artists at the booths. These Americans here pay more for their taxi rides than the locals. They live here, but pay more anyway. They have money, apparently."

"Are we buying anything, Nathan? We really are poor students. And we don't have a car to carry things around."

"Good, not buying is perfect."

I had no idea where we were when the driver let us out. The artist market area had table after table of sculptures, paintings, and books with gringos waiting to sell them. We kept walking to see if anything happened.

"Where are you from?" a man from behind a table asked as we inspected his sculptures.

"I should be asking you," I replied.

"San Bernadino," he answered.

"That's in California. How long have you been here?"

"I retired here," he said. "I've been here five years."

"I guess you like it well enough."

"Yes, I love it. I have no plans on going back. The weather is great, the people friendly, the food is great."

"You don't get hassled by the people? They have attitudes about Americans."

"I get hassled back home. It happens, but I have friends here and a good life."

"Do you make a good living here?"

"Like I say, I am retired. I am an artist and like to sell my paintings for the challenge and the appreciation. San Luis Potosi has a reputation, and we have enough customers from America to make it worth our while. I do well considering I don't need the business."

"Laid back. Sounds great."

"I got tired of the rat race."

"I can understand that."

"What brings you here? You and the lady?"

"We're students and it's spring break."

"Yes, we see quite a few of your ilk. Why aren't you in Miami or Malibu?"

"We want to see the pyramids," Michaela informed him.

"Where are you from, with that accent?"

"Frankfurt, Germany."

"You are German. I would never guess. You look like you're from here."

"I do have beige skin, but I don't look Mexican. No one confuses me on that."

"I suppose not. I wouldn't know where to place you."

"I am Jewish."

"That may make sense. What is a German Jew with beige skin doing in San Luis Potosi?"

"I am studying in Texas now and heard of this place. So we are on our way to see the pyramids, but I am intrigued about your artist colony."

"Well, good for you. I hope you have a nice stay."

"I quite enjoy, as a matter of fact."

"Good luck to the both of you."

"*Ciao*," Michaela said as we walked away.

"I suppose it is a charmed life to be an artist," I commented as we casually walked past other tables. "On the other hand, I hate having to make sales. I'm sure selling your own items is better than selling insurance or used cars."

"I think I would like the interaction with so many people from so many places. Yes, I think they must lead a charmed life. I envy them."

"We need to get moving though, you know. Do you mind? We can still make it to Oaxaca today if we can get to a bus. We've seen enough booths to get the flavor."

"I don't know where the bus station is," she replied. "Let's just start hitchhiking now. Right here at the artist market. There are tourists here. This may be a good place to do so."

"Take charge," I said.

We walked onto the street. As soon as she held out her thumb, a pickup truck stopped.

"Oaxaca," Michaela said to the driver with his window down.

"*Vente* kilometers," he answered her. "No far. So sorry, *señorita*."

"Twenty kilometers is good. Thanks."

"*Mi mujer*," he said pointing to a woman next to him. "Wife."

"*No problema*," Michaela returned. "*Mi amigo* in back."

She pointed to the empty flat bed of the pickup truck. That was to be my place. Just like when I was a kid on our farm.

The ride got us onto the road and out of town. I loved the friendliness Michaela displayed along the way as we rode. I had no idea what they were talking about or how they were communicating, but it added to the confidence and adoration I already felt for her.

We made it to Oaxaca in three more rides. There was even sun left. Enough time to find a cheap hotel.

Chapter 27

"We're not going inside the city itself," Michaela informed me. "There is a site called Monte Alban here in this Oaxacan valley. I just want to see that and move on. I don't care about museums, beaches, restaurants, or anything else while we're here in Mexico. With a few exceptions. The ruins here and in Mexico City are what intrigue me."

"Perfect," I said. "Me too. The Olmec, the Mayan, the Aztec and all. They are special. More than just seeing an Indian reservation."

"When we get to Mexico City though," Michaela continued, "the anthropological museum is important. It is supposed to be one of the best museums in the world, and it is about prehistoric tribal Mexico. But for now, here in Oaxaca, just the pyramid at Monte Alban is enough. We are hitchhiking. We don't have much time."

"So many places in ancient Mexico were suddenly populated and then suddenly abandoned." I recounted the stories I'd heard all my life. "Then another era of population and then abandonment by them. Could be famine, plague, invasions, or whatever, but life was so volatile in this area. How did they get such advanced civilizations with all the turmoil and disruptions?"

"All the theories about space alien invasions," she said with a sigh. "Not that something didn't happen, but it is like they are making a new set of superstitions to fit modern man. Not just the gods with magic wands, but outer space mischief and colonization theories too. Anyway, it is all fascinating. But I want to see the pyramid. Any history they have that has merit is great, and I'll listen to some of the superstition too, just to get a flavor, but the ruin is what is important."

"Well, we're almost to the ruin now," I said while pointing toward the horizon in front of us. "You can see the hills there. One more ride. So look sexy."

"You make me feel cheap, Nathan."

"No, not cheap. We've been through this. We don't want to tease them. But look adorable. Even a woman in a pickup gave us a ride this afternoon. So you're adorable but not cheap. We're both adorable little gringos because of you. So get busy with your adorableness. We're almost there."

Our next ride took us right up to Monte Alban.

"Thank you, Padre," Michaela said to the Catholic priest as he dropped us off.

"I hope you find history. Excuse my speaking. My English is no *bueno*."

"This is exactly what we are here for, Padre. All the history here. *Muchas gracias*."

He nodded his farewell and drove off.

Before we walked farther, we stared at the pyramid in front of us. The Mesoamerican pyramids were smaller than the great pyramids of Giza in Egypt. But they had more character to them, I decided. Whoever built the one at Monte Alban or the ones in Egypt had something in mind, so a direct comparison was not appropriate. But there was as much art to the design here as there was function.

"So," Michaela began as she read through her travel

guide. "It says the city, when this pyramid was built, was part of the Zapotec political and economic center. Monte Alban was the dominant city. There are other ruins around, I don't know how far away. I wish we had a car to be able to see them easily. We could happily spend a few days here, I think."

She read further.

"My goodness, Nathan, we are nearly two kilometers in elevation. The mountains do not look so tall. Just hills, in fact. We have been rising the whole time, apparently. We started where your sister lives, which was near the ocean. And now we are almost two kilometers high."

"That's over a mile high. A mile and a half even. Wow."

"The city, or early settlement, was here around five hundred BC and lasted for over a thousand years. It was very dominant for a while and then disappeared." She looked up at me. "Like you mentioned before, so many of these old empires in the Americas just disappeared. Over and over we keep reading this. Just overnight they disappeared. This one lasted a thousand years, but it sounds like overnight, poof, it just vanished. Then all these theories spring up trying to explain, when we don't have a clue. So now, just the ruins, like this one, are all that's left. And there is no written history from back then to give us clues."

"Okay, let's walk around," I suggested.

"There is a main plaza in the pyramid," she said while reading as we walked. "We can walk to it and look out."

It felt good being in a historical place. But I was frustrated. I wanted to know so much more than was

181

available to us. Who were these people? Where did they come from? Their concept of zero, the era of pyramids, things to identify with civilizations in Asia and Europe. All these mysteries whetted my curiosity even more. It wasn't studying, it was inhaling life.

"We didn't learn much except from my guidebook," Michaela commented as we ended our walk around the grounds. "I can say I've seen it and it was worth it. But I wanted more. A plaque here and a plaque there to give an idea of the history. I know little more from being here than before I came. I guess there is a museum nearby, if we had a car. We don't. Why isn't there more explanation here? Handy information for us on foot. It's probably here somewhere."

"Hey," I said looking at an approaching car. "There's our ride."

"If you are so bold, you ask then."

The car conveniently stopped next to us.

"You look American," the driver said with a Hispanic accent.

"Yes, sir," I replied. "And we need a ride to the main road."

"Let me take some pictures of the pyramid first. I just came from the pyramids near Mexico City. This isn't as good. I won't be long."

"Is there a bus we can catch to Mexico City?" Michaela asked.

"Sure," the man answered. "A town is nearby. It has a bus station."

"Lovely," Michaela chirped as we got into the back seat of his car.

The worst part of our stay at Monte Alban was the cheap hotel we chose in a nearby town. The mattress bedspring squeaked so loudly it sounded like we were having an orgy every time one of us moved. We were more than ready to move on the next morning.

Chapter 28

Eighty percent of the population where I grew up was Hispanic. A large percent spoke Spanish as a mother tongue, with a large percentage of those struggling with the English language. There were as many Spanish-speaking radio and TV stations as there were English-speaking. Before I started elementary school, we had access to only one television station. I would watch with fascination the movies in Spanish from Mexico. Every Sunday, it seemed, they showed the story of Jesus and the crucifixion on the cross. I knew the story of Jesus. Even though the movie was in Spanish, I followed it well. Spanish, in other words, was a major cultural item in my life from the very beginning.

Many aspects of Mexican culture fascinated me. Even more than with the Maya, I was enamored with the Aztec, also called the Mexica. By the time the Spanish arrived in Vera Cruz in 1519, they were the dominant tribe. This story alone, how the Aztec managed pre-Columbian dominance, was inspiring.

The Aztec originated in Canada. For survival they migrated southward. It reminds me of how in the New Testament the least shall be first, for the early Aztec kept getting pushed out of one domain to another. They were eventually shoved down to what is now the Mexico City area, then known as Tenochtitlan. For survival they learned how to fight. As they struggled, they just wanted to be left alone. They consistently improved their numbers and fighting skills, however, until they were good enough to become mercenaries and hired themselves out to surrounding tribes.

And kept getting stronger.

More and more decisively they defeated their enemies. With ever-growing prowess, they pushed back, then took over. Finally, they became the local power.

Mesoamerica had many dominant cultures through the millennia. The Olmec, Mayan, the Zapotec, Totonac, the Teotihuacanos, and Toltecs. These tribes and civilizations borrowed from each other. The Aztec took from their predecessors, both in histories and myths, and made much of them their own. By the sixteenth century they had an elaborate mythological system that had them at the center of the universe with an illustrious past.

There was much to admire about the Aztec, I decided. No matter the borrowed civilization and history they thrust upon themselves. And in spite of the savagery they imposed in battle or, as rulers, upon their subjects.

When the Spanish first entered their realm in the sixteenth century, they beheld a culture with elaborate science, agriculture, and mathematics. By then the Aztec had an elaborate economy based on trade. They produced their own calendar system as well. The earliest Spanish compared the Aztec capital to Constantinople.

But the harsh life the Aztec knew as they formed and grew put a dark side to them as well as this elaborate civilization. The mercenary existence that gained them strength and power became a morbid center for their religious beliefs. Somehow they determined that if their god of war, which was also their god of the sun, did not get enough blood every day, it might lose the eternal fight with the dark forces of the universe. These warrior people fought even when peace was at hand, just to gain prisoners to sacrifice to this god. This would give him the strength to reappear every morning and start a new day. The Aztec inherited human sacrifice from the Mayan and other tribes, but they put their unique stamp on it through their morbid religion.

The other tribes hated the Aztec as a result. The Aztec had allies, but even they were leery of them. It is better to be an ally than an enemy, but life was not good either way.

I was glad Michaela and I had Oaxaca out of the way. It was the Aztec and Mayan ruins we wanted to see. These were the people that fascinated me since my early Texas childhood. Their pyramids of grandeur were close by to help share their glorious past, with their ruins in modern-day Mexico City, ruins more glorious than those at Monte Alban, and with a history that had me enamored beyond measure.

Chapter 29

Mexico City was a nightmare—eight million people crammed together in the middle of the country. The only thing I got out of being there was the anthropological museum. I'd heard a great deal about this museum and wanted to know, for my own satisfaction, that I had seen it in my life. I adored Mexico for having such a museum, a pride they displayed rightly.

Our major objective for the entire trip was the pyramid complex twenty-five miles north of Mexico City. It was good they were north of the city. It meant we were officially on our way back home to Texas as we left the city behind. A scenic way back home. Not just traveling back to Texas, but gawking our way back.

"I get shivers, Michaela," I said with awe. "These pyramids are so beautiful. This whole complex is. But the pyramid of the sun and the pyramid of the moon especially. They mean more to me than the pyramids of Giza. I don't mean to compare. I've never been to Giza. I don't really know which are more impressive or significant. I'm just in awe, and I'm from here, or not so far away. The gringo world I live in is far removed, I suppose, from this one in Mesoamerica. But still, I grew up right on the border where most of our population had roots in Mexico. So some of this rubbed off on me."

"They are magnificent," she assured. "Beautiful. I never saw the pyramids at Giza either, so I cannot say if they look more impressive, but these are wonderful."

"There is so much to the religions of Mesoamerica. And so many of them seem to overlap. No matter who conquered who through the millennia, the conqueror regarded all the gods and histories and legends of the conquered as their own. So many anthropologists and archaeologists are filtering through it all now trying to decide who did what or invented what legend."

Michaela began to read through her travel guide as if on cue.

"It talks about murals here," she began, informing as she read along. "Let's don't get so caught up in the pyramids themselves that we pass up these murals and whatever else. Let's really comb the area. We may never come back here, so let's do it right."

She continued to read.

"So this is the exact setting of Teotihuacan, the center of the Mesoamerican universe, so to speak. Yes, these pyramids are more significant than Monte Alban and, for that matter, all the other pyramids in Mesoamerica. Right here. We are here at the best and most significant site of pre-Columbian architecture and importance. This is also the largest city in antiquity for Mesoamerica. It covered eight square miles."

"Can you imagine the Spanish when they saw all this? Cortez, Hernando Cortez, you know. All these backward savages he expected to see. Except they built an architectural complex and society as sophisticated and brilliant as any in Europe."

"My goodness, Nathan, Teotihuacan at its peak was thought to have been the sixth largest city in the entire world. And they didn't just dig for grubworms for existence. They had a sophisticated and scientific elite.

With advanced tools. Not from iron or metal, but obsidian. Volcanic residue, you know. Very durable and incredibly sharp."

"They had multistory buildings, I heard."

"Yes, that's right. It says that here. We use cranes for those. I don't know how they would have accomplished theirs. Maybe platforms. Anyway, they built these complicated buildings."

"The Aztec considered this place the birthplace of the gods," I related.

"Somehow, they never heard of Mt. Olympus," she joked. "It's so fascinating to see the overlap of the human mind. It's like we are all related after all."

"They had an advanced economy," I added. "With a network of roads for intermingling goods and culture. For peaceful purposes. They didn't just conquer and fight. They were adept at trade. Theories in modern economics tout the importance of trade, even more than military might, for stability and peace. They had that here."

"There are signs that trade from here reached as far away as Vera Cruz," she read further. "Maybe beyond."

"The law of economic interdependency," I stated as I thought back to my studies in economics at Texas A&M.

"More than pyramids here, Nathan. There is so much history, whether we see it all or not. The complex here is just the book cover."

She read more.

"But it was the class differences that did them in," she continued. "That doesn't mean everyone has to be equal. It says the elitism, religious elistism mostly, from what I read, the priestly, was their downfall. Different status and class can be a norm, but elitism got out of hand here. More than just economic elitism, but religious and political division as well. When severe drought hit or some other catastrophe, it pushed these differences to the extreme. No more cohesion. Or not enough."

She closed her book.

"This would be the Avenue of the Dead in front of us," she mused. "Four kilometers long, forty meters wide. So meticulously laid out. It contains the massive Pyramid of the Sun, third largest pyramid in the world, and the Pyramid of the Moon. These were to the sun and moon gods. Part of the set-up is like a solar calendar. I guess like Stonehenge, but in this case, as part of the city landscape and make-up. There is this spirit-of-man thing, Nathan. I feel related to them even as I feel so distant from them. We're alike in so many ways. Not just different."

"They had a feathered serpent god," I commented.

"Yes, Quetzalcoatl. God of wind, agriculture, fertility, rain, and justice, all the civilized concepts of a god, I guess. He created mankind and the world, as well as the creator of the arts. He was the most important god to the Aztec. He taught mankind how to measure time and gave the calendar. What is significant about this god is the Emperor Moctezuma believed in his return."

"This Moctezuma guy is who we gringos call Montezuma. As in the 'Marine Corps Hymn.' The guy in our fight song you might say. 'From the halls of Montezuma,' you know. Well, here we the hell are. Where are my Marine buds to celebrate?"

"So this Quetzalcoatl was the god of the resurrection of the dead. He went to the underworld, to their version of Hell, I just read. He is identified with Venus, the evening and morning star. Brilliant in the sky, but lowers to Hell, gathers the bones of the dead, anoints them with his blood, and creates mankind. He never required human sacrifice. He was expelled by the god of the night sky. So, the Aztec chief that Cortez met, this Montezuma guy you have in the 'Marine Corps Hymn,' thought it was the return of Quetzalcoatl. As if 'We're saved,' you know. 'The good times have returned.' "

"Boy, was he fatally wrong," I said with a sigh as I shook my head. "Waiting for a savior. Wow. Just like the Bible in so many ways. Except fatally different. This is indeed so intriguing in whatever comparison. The human soul in search. Such a connection with our ancient world. Spooky. Some universal spiritual DNA going on here."

"Aren't you glad we spent our spring break here, Nathan? We're students. We're on more than a break now. You used to study on your spring break before, to catch up with your coursework. This is the best course we could take, though. A huge classroom right here with us to study and marvel at."

"*Genau*," I answered.

Chapter 30

"We're passing through a rainforest," I mused.
"That's what this is. We've been in it for an hour. I've
been to Hawaii and was in a tropical rainforest there. But
this is bigger. It's so great to know some are left."

"It is such a beautiful country," Michaela
commented. "I didn't think about going through a
tropical rainforest. But here we are."

"I wonder when we'll get to Vera Cruz," I mused.
"That's where Cortez entered Mexico. I'm not trying to
dwell on history. Here we are passing through paradise,
but his landing was so significant. All this comes to mind
as we see more of Mexico. Cortez entered Mexico at
Vera Cruz in the early sixteenth century. He met
Montezuma, then took over. Changed everything. We
keep hearing about how America stole land from the
Indians. Like we gringos did all this and Vietnam too or
whatever. But Russia took over Alaska, then parts of
California. Japan got into the act in Asia. China became
the China of today when the Chin took over the rest of
what we know today as China. So here I am thinking of
all this because we're on our way to Vera Cruz. Vera
Cruz spurred a chain of events in my mind trail now. So
many interconnections in our world."

"Enjoy the scenery," she chided. "It is better."
"Yeah."
"And another subject is at hand, Nathan. Do you see

the bus driver? And his assistant. I guess his assistant. He sits just behind him and has a money bag and a ledger."

"What about them?" I asked as I focused now on the two operating our bus.

"They keep looking at us. Like they are checking us out. I think it is more than curiosity."

"We are the only two gringos on the bus. I guess they get bored. I hope they don't sing now. They're both so overweight. I mean like letting themselves go, you know. Like who cares. Okay. But also shaved heads. Not macho manly, so I'm thinking. Planned cosmetics by them. It's like they have a manual on how to be ugly."

The assistant walked over to us and looked first at Michaela and then at me.

"Americano?" he asked.

"Yes," I replied.

"*¿Hablas Español?*"

I knew what he was asking, but my Spanish wasn't good enough to have a good conversation, so I shrugged my shoulders to indicate I didn't understand.

"Speak English?" he asked.

"English, yes," I replied.

"My English very bad," he said slowly and with a struggle. "Hello."

"Hi," I greeted back.

"Hello," Michaela replied.

"We go Vera Cruz. You go?"

"Yes," I replied. "We go to Vera Cruz."

"You stay there?"

"Just tonight. We go to Texas."

"You from Texas?"

"Yes."

"Very good. I work Texas before. Illegal. I pick

cotton on farm. Summer. Hot."

"I wonder if he worked in the fields where I grew up," I said in a whisper to Michaela. "We had the earliest cotton season in the country. The only area that harvested in summers."

"Where stay in Vera Cruz?" he asked further.

"Hotel," I answered.

"What hotel?"

I shrugged again.

"I show you good hotel. We arrive Vera Cruz one hour. I show you." He then glanced at the bus driver. "We show you hotel."

"Thanks," I replied.

"Near bus station. How you get to Texas?"

"Bus."

"I show you."

"Thanks."

He went back to his seat, then picked up the guitar and began to strum. I turned to look at the faces of the other passengers. They continued their stares out the windows obliviously.

Soon he bellowed out a song in Spanish. He was barely more than monotone. He then began talking to the bus driver in a very loud, boisterous voice. As if showing off. Or so it seemed to me.

All the bus driver characters on this trip seemed to live in their own world, as if competing with one another as to who was the most obnoxious. I felt too self-conscious to mock another culture, but no matter how much I got after myself, they came across as one big joke, worthy of Hollywood.

The assistant walked over to me again.

"You know play guitar?" he asked.

I stared cautiously at him, then nodded yes.

"Sing, please." He looked toward the passengers. "We want gringo to sing."

He practically shoved the guitar at me. Michaela looked on while wearing a humored expression. She nodded that I should do so.

I took his guitar.

"What you sing?" he asked.

"The Beatles," I replied.

Even Michaela looked surprised at my choice.

"What song, Nathan?" she asked.

"*Girl*," I answered. "And it's to you."

"You know how to play this song?"

"It's easy. And I love the words. John Lennon wrote it for me to sing to you, in fact. Ha. So. Good a place as any."

She glowed approvingly.

I strummed the opening two lines several times to find my key for this guitar. I then looked down at the guitar and began to sing.

"Bravo, *amigo*," many of the passengers cheered after I finished.

I was almost grateful to the guy for his guitar now.

"Nathan, that was wonderful!" Michaela swooned. "I have heard you sing since our days in Israel, but somehow that was the best I ever heard you. Maybe because of circumstances. But it was wonderful."

The assistant took back the guitar firmly. He remained quiet the rest of the ride.

It was dark by the time we arrived at the bus station in Vera Cruz. I hoped for the driver and his assistant to go about their business, but they immediately approached us again as we got off the bus.

195

"Come," the driver said, leading us out to the sidewalk in front of the bus station.

"We need a bus," I informed him.

"Too late now. Come. We find you hotel. But first we have beer."

"No, we're tired," I insisted.

"No, no, *amigo*. One beer."

I looked at Michaela. She didn't seem to like the idea, but walked behind them out into the street. I followed.

"You like Mexico?" the driver asked as he led us into a bar.

"It's very pretty," Michaela answered. "And historical."

"Why you come here?" the assistant asked.

"Wait, have beer first," the driver said as we approached the bar.

"Mexican beer," the assistant instructed. "Mexican beer best. Better than America."

Michaela and I both nodded.

A loud and vocal competition began between the two again in Spanish as we sipped on the beers they ordered. We seemed there solely for their amusement. Or some fantasy they had.

"Have more beer," the driver pushed. "You feel good when you sleep. More beer."

I looked at Michaela and smirked. We might as well go along, I decided. They were entertaining, in fact, in a pathetic way.

"More beer," the assistant bellowed while shoving two more beers toward us.

"I don't feel so good now, Nathan," Michaela said with a grimace.

"Last one, *amigo*," I told the driver firmly. "We need a hotel."

"Hotel near. Last beer. Drink."

I began to worry as I saw how timidly Michaela was downing her beer.

"That's enough," I said firmly. "We must go."

"One beer, *amigo*," they said in unison.

"No," I answered. "My friend doesn't feel good."

I took her by the arm and led her outside.

"I'm sorry, Michaela. They were showing off and I let them. I was bugged, but it was funny too. I took them too lightly. They are weird enough, but the fastest way to get in trouble is to underestimate your opponent."

"I'm feeling sick, Nathan. I can't go on."

I walked her to a hotel a few feet away.

"I'll get us a room. I've got the money belt. We'll have to spend a bit. We've been living cheap. It's a nice hotel but not luxury. We'll splurge tonight."

"I can't go on, Nathan."

"They were trying to get us drunk. I should have walked out sooner."

"I need to sit down while you get the room."

"Sit down on the curb. The hotel entrance is behind you. I'll be quick."

I watched Michaela struggle to sit on the curb, then lean over as if ready to puke. I rushed inside the hotel feeling guilty.

"A double room," I told the clerk.

"Double, *si, señor*. How many nights?"

"Just tonight."

I turned to check on Michaela and saw she wasn't at the curb anymore. I walked back out of the hotel. She was nowhere to be found. Frantically, I looked up and down the sidewalk. Nowhere. I feared the worst and rushed back into the hotel.

"Where are your police?" I asked the clerk.

"Police? Is something wrong, *señor*?"

"My friend is missing. A girl. She was sick and I left her on the curb just here. And now she's gone."

"Perhaps she lays down somewhere."

"I looked all around. I need the police. Can you help?"

"Let me call them, *señor*. Just a moment."

While he called, I searched outside once more. Still nothing. Panic welled up inside me.

"Can you direct me to the police station, please?" I asked on my return.

"I will have someone go with you. It is not far from here."

The young man who accompanied me to the police station spoke no English. I was glad. I was too frustrated for small talk.

Inside the police station was a man behind a desk wearing a khaki uniform. He was the only man in the front room. I heard the hotel assistant talking to him in Spanish and recognized just enough to gather that my wife was missing and that I only spoke English. The hotel clerk then smiled at me with a nod and left. The policeman looked at me with disdain.

"I speak a little English," the policeman said coldly. "Can I help you?"

"I just arrived in Vera Cruz by bus. The bus driver and his assistant were to show my girlfriend and me where we could get a cheap room. First, they got us drunk. We left them after my girlfriend started feeling bad. Ready to puke."

The policeman broke into a grin when I mentioned how we got drunk.

"Since my girlfriend wasn't feeling well, I left her at the curb in front of the hotel while I went inside to get us a room."

"You left your *mujer* out in the street and went to the hotel?" he asked incredulously.

"She's not my wife," I corrected him. "We didn't mean to get drunk. I think the bus driver and his assistant did it on purpose. They wanted my girlfriend for themselves, I think."

"Are you blaming your problem on the bus drivers?"

"I'm relating what happened. I'm not blaming anyone. But they did want us drunk."

"Why did you get drunk with them if you are so suspicious?"

"I went along with it thinking we could handle it. But I was wrong."

The policeman grimaced and turned away in disgust.

"It sounds like you haven't heard of a missing girl tonight," I said forcefully, showing my frustration.

"No, *señor*, there is no missing girl reported."

"Can you put out an alert?"

"Is she missing, *señor*? Or just not with you?"

I could feel the hate inside. The words to the Bob Dylan song "Just Like Tom Thumb's Blues" were blasting in my mind. The line about how the cops don't need you and expected the same in return. The setting of the song was even Mexico, though Juarez instead of Vera Cruz.

"She was sick and we needed a room," I said to the policeman. "I was just a few feet away, trying to get us a room."

"And you turned around and she was gone," he replied with a smirk.

"Can you put out an alert?" I repeated.

"How do you know she is missing, *señor*?"

"Are you not going to put out an alert?"

"I can put out an alert that an American woman is lost," he said. "Is she white like you or Mexican-American?"

"She is white, but her skin is darker than mine. Some might think her Mexican."

"That does not help us, *señor*."

"Can you put out an alert?"

"I will put out an alert. Good luck. Where can I find you?"

I thought about his question. There was no way I could stay in Vera Cruz. It was getting late, and Vera Cruz was a big town. I needed to head for the border. I was nervous to leave, but I couldn't see staying. Nothing was going to come of this alert thing with the cop.

"This is the hotel I was talking about," I said to the cop as I handed him a piece of paper where I wrote the name. "I'll leave word that you will notify them if you find anything."

"We will contact you if we find her," he replied while I walked out of the police station.

As much as I hated the bus driver crew, I hated myself more. This was amateur on my part to let this happen to us.

"Did you find your *mujer, señor*?" the hotel clerk asked as I walked up to the counter.

"It sounds like she didn't make her way here while I was gone," I said nervously.

"No, *señor*. She did not come here."

I thought frantically.

"Do you have something I can write on?" I asked him.

"Paper here."

"Pen?"

He handed me a pen, and I wrote my mother's name and phone number.

"This is how you can reach me in Texas," I said. "And here's my name. My first name anyway. I'm Nathan."

"*Bueno, señor*."

"I am on my way to Texas. I will call this number I just gave you along the way in case my friend comes here. It's my mother's phone number, and she'll keep me informed if you call. If my friend returns here, I have all the money. Please let her stay somewhere here. We'll find a way to pay you."

"*Si, señor*."

"My friend Michaela knows my mother's phone number in case of emergency. She will need to call her."

"Of course. Good luck to you."

I walked along the street as I held out my thumb. Occasionally I looked around just to get an idea of my chances for a ride.

"American?" a voice from a car asked me.

A mustachioed man was at the steering wheel of an old American car.

"I am trying to get to Texas," I told him.

"*Si*. I take you to highway."

"Yeah? Great. But first, where can I find a telephone? I need to call Texas."

"Telephone? You need telephone?"

201

"Yes."

"I take you. Get in car."

I put mine and Michaela's backpacks into his rear seat and got in next to him.

"There is telephone place near. I take you. International telephone."

"Thanks. Thank you so much."

I explained in very slow English about my problem as he drove us. He nodded that he understood.

"Here is telephone place," he said as we got out of his car to walk in. "Many telephones here. You have cash for telephone?"

I had not thought of that in my haste.

"Just a little," I replied. "*Poquito*."

"It okay. I have money. I help you."

It was like God sent him. With all the bad luck lately, I couldn't believe such kindness.

The lines were so busy the man could not get through. And when he did, the operator could not place the call to my mother successfully at first. The man stayed with me the entire two hours it took to reach my mother by telephone. Any anger or frustration I had at having to go through a third world setting went out the window just from this man's kindness and patience.

"Here, *amigo*," he said to me as he handed me the telephone. "It good now. Your mother talking now."

I wanted to hug him as I grabbed the phone.

"Mother!" I exclaimed.

"Nathan, is that you? What on earth are you doing? What is going on?"

"I'm in Vera Cruz and I've lost Michaela."

"What?"

"Yes, it's a long story. Michaela got sick and we had

to get a hotel room. I left her on the curb in front of the hotel. She was ready to puke. I went in to get us a room, and when I came back she was gone. I reported it to the police and they didn't know anything of her whereabouts. So, I'm going to call the hotel and then start hitchhiking home. If Michaela calls you, that's where I'm headed. Tell her to wait on me at the McAllen border where my car is. I have all the money and passports. Just know this is happening. I have to go now. I don't have money for this call."

"Nathan, what kind of call is this?"

"I'm sorry to worry you, but I have to go. I'm heading home now. Just tell Michaela to meet me at the McAllen border crossing. That's where my car is."

"Yes, your car is with your sister in McAllen."

"Handle all calls from Michaela if you get them. She will head to McAllen, I'm sure."

"Yes, of course. My goodness, what a mess. This is serious."

"I hate worrying you like this, but I have to go."

"Yes, hurry home."

The man who had helped me was still there for further assistance if I needed.

"Can you call this hotel number?" I asked. "The hotel just now where you picked me up."

He nodded yes and proceeded to call. Soon he handed the phone back to me.

"This is the American that was at your hotel," I said into the phone. "Have you heard anything about her?"

"No. No. *Nada*. Nothing."

"If you hear from her, tell her to go to McAllen. My sister will help. I am on my way."

"McAllen. I say this to your wife. Good luck."

"Thank you."

Such kindness reassured me. I loved loving Mexico again.

Chapter 31

The man who had helped with the telephone call drove me to the edge of Vera Cruz on the main highway to Texas, toward my boyhood home in the lower Rio Grande Valley of Texas. My fears were soothed by the kindness he displayed. It was late at night, and I didn't have a clue where I was except north of Vera Cruz on the way home.

Hitchhiking can suck in Texas. I had no idea what to expect about Mexico. I tried not to think about it because it was something I had to do and it was probably faster than riding a bus.

The lack of traffic looked serious, however. Maybe it would get better in the morning, but I was determined to get home tonight.

I am not a cool, calm, take-life-as-it-comes kind of guy. I do not know how I made it in the Marines, much less backpacking around the world, because I get frustrated very quickly. I had no watch on me as I waited. It seemed like an hour without even a hint of a ride. Hardly anyone was on this highway.

The stars were out. The last thing I wanted to see were the stars. I was in no mood for sentimental memories of my precious Michaela. But they smiled at me as I waited. She was there with me somehow, and it warmed me. The full depth of her beauty and charm was inside of me, reminding me that we were going to see each other again. That this was one more episode in our glorious and eventful time together. Even though apart.

A car drove by me very slowly as if checking me out. I had seen this car just a few minutes before, coming from the other direction. Was this a potential ride, or something more ominous for which to be fearful?

"Are you American?" a male's voice asked from inside the car. The accent was not strongly Hispanic.

"Yes."

"Are you going to the border?"

"Yes."

"It is late at night. It is dangerous for you here. Why don't you take a bus?"

"I don't have enough money."

"Why would an American, a white American, come to Mexico with so little money? And then have to hitchhike back home? This is not wise, my friend."

"It wasn't very wise," I concurred.

"Be careful. Good luck."

In a few minutes the same car drove by again to stop a few feet in front of me.

"My friend," he said, "I am concerned for your safety."

He reached inside his shirt pocket and pulled out a badge.

"I work with the Federalis. You probably know of the Federalis."

I nodded that I did as I studied him.

"I hope you can trust me, because I want to help you. Please get in. It is three in the morning. You are not going to get a ride at this hour on this road. Let me take you home with me. I will put you in a better spot tomorrow. Or better yet, I will buy you a bus ticket."

"Buses are so slow. I am in a hurry."

"Are you a student?"

"Yes."

"I went to the University of Southern California. That is why my English is so good."

USC is an expensive private school, I mused. This guy must be well off.

"Please trust me," he repeated. "I want to help you. Get in. I will take you home."

I picked up the two backpacks and got in.

"Is this your spring break?"

"Yes. I'm on the way back now."

"And penniless. He comes to a third world country with no money, gets stranded, and can't even help out our impoverished country by spending anything." He gave a chuckle as he shook his head.

"If you are a Federali, do you think you can help me out? I have a problem."

"I can't keep you out of jail, if that's what you mean."

"No, I was with a girl. She's from Germany. She was a student with me, and it was her idea to come to Mexico. She wanted to see the pyramids. That's why I did this. But we got separated in Vera Cruz. I called my mother, and there is no word of her still. So I don't know if she's okay. Is there any way you can find out?"

"Not at three in the morning. We will do a search for her tomorrow. You need a good night's sleep. I am glad I found you first. There are people who are not so generous."

This didn't reassure my fears for Michaela.

Chapter 32

"So where are you calling from now?" my mother asked.

"The bus station in Reynosa," I replied.

"Thank God you made it there."

"I had some luck."

"Well, they found Michaela. She's waiting for you at the Border Patrol in Reynosa. No, not the Border Patrol. She's at Mexico's immigration office, just before the bridge. She'll be with their immigration people."

"Thank God she's okay."

"She's not just okay, she's in good spirits. All chipper. Like nothing happened."

A broad smile spread across my face. *That's my Michaela.*

I was still tense by the time I entered the border crossing. But there she was, chatting with a lady and her son at immigration. I watched her for a moment to let it sink in that our nightmare was over. She caught a glimpse of me, and her demeanor turned to remorse.

"Is there anything we need besides passports?" I asked our customs officer at a desk near the entrance. "I'm a citizen, I have my driver's license, actually."

"That will do, sir," he replied. "Does the lady have a passport?"

Without answering, I pulled out her passport and my license from the money belt I wore. The officer inspected them and waved us through. As simple as that.

"Are you okay?" I asked her as we began our walk across the international bridge.

"I am quite tired. I had luck in getting here, but it was still a hassle."

"You make your own luck, Michaela. It would have been more than just a hassle to anyone but you."

"Is that a compliment? You seem stressed."

"I am very stressed. I'm glad it all worked out, though. I was worried sick. So many things could have happened."

"So many things did happen."

"Yeah, but you know what I mean."

"Yes, I certainly know what you mean. I am glad we got to see the pyramids for all the adventure we lived. But now the adventure is part of our experience too. As if we planned such mischief, or the gods planned for us."

"Yeah. Yeah. I hope I don't have all these memories every time I see a picture of those pyramids. The Aztecs sacrificed humans at the altars of those pyramids by the tens of thousands. That's depressing enough. Now I have all these personal memories of my own."

"Nathan," she said as she stopped to pull me by the arm. "These will be precious memories for us someday. You were my companion the whole time. Even when we were physically separated. I felt the bond inside with you. It gave me courage."

I melted right in front of her. It didn't seem corny at all as I listened. It seemed a continuation of everything she meant to me.

"I want to make love to you right here," I said as I reached over to hug her.

"Then let's do that. As soon as we get home. It was

an exciting week, but all the more now I just want to be a normal person living a normal life."

"I hope you get that normal life, Michaela, but you will never be a normal person."

"I think another compliment."

"Can you talk about it? What all happened to you?"

"I am still living it emotionally right now, Nathan. Let me breathe again first, I think. I don't know when I can talk about it. Maybe in the car. We have a long drive ahead of us, and I am so tired. And you? Are you able to drive us back to College Station?"

"Six hours' drive before we get home. I'll make it, but I'll need to stop for coffee and refreshment along the way."

"Likewise, me. Let me sleep on the way. But you used the word 'home.' We're going home now. That is so reassuring to me. Home with you. Such a beautiful thought. If you need me to help you stay awake, I can do this. But I need some sleep, if possible."

Everything returned to a calm about us as we waited for my sister to take us to her apartment. Our adventures and peril were never brought up as she drove us. Probably by design. We all wanted our lives back. The wonderful boring ones we used to take for granted.

"We didn't make it to Padre Island, did we?" Michaela asked, her disappointment evident as we began our journey back home. "I so wanted to see this beautiful place as you described it, Nathan. I hope we make it there someday."

She lay down with her head on my lap, her feet dangling off to the floorboard of the passenger side of the car. I could feel my hormones flowing.

Much of our travel was across the King Ranch, one

long huge stretch lasting more than an hour, a ranch so big the cowboys herded at times by helicopter. I was proud of the King Ranch, the largest in the continental United States.

Just past the King Ranch was a Border Patrol station, a check stop to see if there were illegal aliens in any of the vehicles. I had to wake Michaela for this.

"Where are you headed?" the Border Patrol agent asked me.

"College Station," I replied.

"Do you have anything to report? Are you both US citizens? Have you recently been to Mexico and are you carrying any goods you need to declare?"

"We have nothing to declare," I told him.

Michaela struggled from her sleep. Finally, she sat up and looked at the agent.

"I am German," she told him.

"Do you have your passport?"

She looked at me for her answer.

"I have it in my money belt," I told the agent.

I pulled it out and handed it to him. He inspected it, then looked briefly at her. He seemed ready to ask another question, but handed back her passport instead.

"Enjoy your trip," he said while turning to leave. "Drive safely."

Michaela stared at me, showing confusion as I continued my drive.

"What was that about?" she asked.

"There are only a couple of highways from my part of Texas to anywhere else. It makes it difficult to sneak illegal aliens into the state. After about a hundred miles they have a second border check, besides the one on the Rio Grande, which is the real border between Texas and

Mexico. It's like at the customs we went through at the border except it's a hundred miles inland. They'll confiscate any contraband you have and apprehend any illegals they find. Sometimes they check your trunk to be sure. It's at random. But they ask you and hold you legally to what you tell them. I'm glad we had your passport."

"Yes, I am very glad of that. I would hate to be arrested."

I looked at her quizzically.

"Are you fit enough to tell me about what happened when we got split up in Vera Cruz?"

She thought for a moment.

"I wish I didn't have to. But I've rested some and will try. It is bad memories for me, Nathan. It will be hard to talk about. I know I should, and I want to be fair to you."

This sounded deep.

"You didn't get raped, did you?" I asked her. "I don't want to pry."

She shook her head no.

"That is almost a lie. But no, I didn't get raped."

She stared straight ahead out the window as I drove along. I regretted I'd asked her. She took a deep breath, then began.

"I wonder if those two bus driver guys that took us to Vera Cruz drugged us. They kept pushing us to drink."

"Wait a minute, wait a minute," I groaned. "Those bus drivers were long gone. We left them at that bar. Why are you bringing them up?"

She shook her head no. "They followed us."

"Oh, God," I moaned. "I'm going to be sick. Better yet, I feel like turning this car around and hunting them down and beating the total crap out of them."

"No, I don't ever want to go back there. Maybe Mexico someday. But let me heal first. I did love our trip. But right now, these memories are not good."

"I am going to beat the total crap out of them. Somehow I am going to pulverize them."

"No, Nathan. Forget this Marine stuff or this Texas stuff. I don't want to think about them anymore except to tell this story and then don't ask me again."

I wasn't convinced. I still wanted to track them down.

"Nathan," she continued, "let me talk."

I nodded, though I wore a defiant sneer.

"I felt dizzy," she began her explanation. "Maybe it was just the beer. If they had drugged me, they would have also drugged you."

"I'll repeat," I said angrily. "The best way to lose a war is to take your opponent for granted. To take them lightly. I ought to know this by now, but they seemed the biggest jokes in the world. Laughable, not dangerous. I took those goons for granted. As too stupid to be harmful."

"Those are the most dangerous," she concurred. "Yes, like you said. We took them for granted. A big, stupid joke. We have traveled so much together. We should have known better."

"This scares me. This taking for granted scares me. I knew better, to always be ready for the unexpected."

"The whole time we were with them on the bus it seemed like we didn't exist to them except for their own benefit. Those two losers needed each other to build each other's egos, like who was the coolest. They had each other to convince them how cool they were. They didn't need the rest of the world to remind them they were losers. The rest of the world didn't exist except to make a joke about. With them as the heroes."

"Did they rape you, Michaela? You can tell me."

"No, Nathan. I would tell you. You would be the one I would want to tell. I was feeling sick and almost vomited. I could even hear you in the hotel trying to get us a room, but I couldn't move. Then someone grabbed me. I don't know how I got loose. But I was desperate. Mother Nature provides us with strength we don't know we have, it seems. Bigger than their egos, I had Mother Nature. I squirmed trying to get loose of his grip. I'm not sure which one grabbed me. I took a self-defense course while a student in Freiburg. I hit one of them in the face with my elbow. The one on my right. He didn't let go, but he jerked when I hit him. I then hit him in the groin with my fist. He let go for just a second."

"How did I not hear any of this?"

"Because they already started dragging me."

"And no one helped you?"

"I don't know if anyone saw. I don't know if anyone was around. It all happened so quickly, with them grabbing me. And I felt so sick. I only wanted to recover. That's why I didn't scream when they grabbed me. You would have heard my scream, but I was sick and all I could think to do was hit. I am small and was drunk. I hit just to distract them. Then hit again in their tender area. I hurt him. I got away. Then I ran. Just ran. I struggled so to run. They panicked and ran the other way. I ran to a house. Everything was closed. Businesses, houses, all closed. But I found a house on the next block with a light on and started banging on the door."

"Thank God."

"Yes, that is how I thought. Thank God. The door opened and a middle-aged lady was at the door showing concern—who was banging on her door, you know?"

"She was brave to open the door."

"Yes, very brave. Someone asleep might have ignored the banging on the door or had a weapon. But she saw me and how frightened I was. And an American too, or whatever she thought. Not normal circumstances. She brought me inside her house and locked the door. She put some blankets on her kitchen floor for me to sleep. I never saw her husband or family. Somehow, she was alone. I was almost scared for her if the two goons, as you call them, were to come back. But I did feel safe. I saw them run away, so I felt safe."

"I know things like this happen," I said with a sigh. "But I just don't understand it. How do goons exist? What the hell do they think? Some simple pleasure just for them? No other element in the universe. Just their pleasure."

"Losers need egos to compensate for their poor self-image," she mused. "Anyway, I had no money or passport, so had to hitchhike. But I was still hoping I could find you. Early the next morning this woman fed me and put me on a bus that took me to a road outside of Vera Cruz. She gave me a little money, pesos, to buy food along the way. I was on the road to the Texas border. That direction, I mean. The way to get there from Vera Cruz. I didn't hitchhike yet because I hoped to see you. That maybe you too would get to this road from Vera Cruz to Texas and we could be together again. But after two hours I knew you weren't coming. I had to decide something, and it seemed you weren't coming. So finally, I began to hitchhike."

215

"My God. My God! How did you make it back alive? But the reason you didn't find me is because I was already gone. Probably on that very road. I also had good luck and helpful people. I want to hear your story first, though. But I'm so glad people helped us. Mexico has so many good people, and I'm glad we met them. We will have good memories of the people."

"Yes, Nathan, what you say is true. But I met some more bad ones."

"God, I hate this. I'm sure you did, but I hate this. God! What happened next, then?"

"A lorry stopped to pick me up. A big lorry driver. It made me nervous, but I had no choice. No money, no passport, no you. Maybe the driver is going far. Maybe I am safe somehow. I had to try."

"A truck driver is unpredictable. A lot of them are from poor families and very sympathetic to people down and out. But a lot of them are gruff and earthy. Bad earthy. Not just good ole boys."

"He was not a good ole boy. He was very friendly in the beginning, but he must have known what he wanted. Because after an hour he began to slow down. There was nowhere to go, but he slowed down. No town, no service place. Why was he slowing down? I knew why. He slowed to turn down a small dirt road. He wasn't stopping to let me out. He was going to take me some place. A place I didn't want to go. So just before he turned, I opened the door and jumped out and started running. Running so far, I hoped, that he couldn't get out of the truck in time to chase me. I ran back to the highway. With the first car I saw, I started waving my hands. Not stick out my thumb like an American, but waving my hands like this was an emergency."

"Which it was. And then what?"

"And then what, ha. I got immediately a ride. But this one also tried to turn off to a side road after a while. I jumped out just like with the lorry driver. I waved my hands again when I got to the highway and got another ride. The same exact thing happened. I was an expert now at jumping out of cars and lorries to the highway. Finally, I got a ride from a very nice and caring man. He was so worried about me. He took me to his town. No turning off the highway. He took me to the bus station and bought me a ticket for Reynosa. I remembered we crossed into Mexico at Reynosa. So I knew you would be there eventually."

"You even beat me back. You're a better hitchhiker than I am. Except for nearly getting raped. I had all the money, but not enough to get back on the bus. Anyway, I had a guy put me up for the night. A Federali. Later an oil worker picked me up. Middle class. He gave me money and wished me luck."

"So many good people, Nathan. And we met them."

"I love you, Michaela. I mean totally. You are the love of my life. I want to marry you. I told you I wasn't ready to get married. I want to marry you anyway. You are my soulmate."

"Yes, Nathan. We are soulmates. That is certain. But you are not ready to get married. Just more in love. With me. I am grateful for that. But you are not ready to get married and neither am I. I am going back home soon to finish my degree, and then I want to go to Africa. Same plan as every time we talk about loving and wanting to marry. We have our other reality. The real one. School and then Africa is my goal. When I get my degree, I will look for work with a German organization that will send

217

me there to Africa. I want to teach English in schools. It is cheap to live there, so I don't have to make much money. Come visit me there. Then we will talk about marriage."

Chapter 33

"Will you be able to take me to the airport?" Michaela asked as we ate supper.

"It's next Thursday. I have a class that afternoon. We have a test the next day. I need to study. I'm not complaining. Just thinking out loud. I keep up with my classes, and I'll make it back from the airport before dark. I can go over everything again when I get back. If I can concentrate. Finals are soon."

"I know it's an inconvenience. I can take the bus, but I wanted to say goodbye."

"I want to say goodbye too. Of course I'll take you."

"I hate the thought of writing," she then said in afterthought. "We'll want to stay in contact, but writing is such a tease. After all this time spent together, and soon it's down to, '*Things went great today. Thinking of you, Sweetheart.*' But it's all we have."

"I'm almost glad I have finals coming," I answered. "Pressure to study. Grades to worry about. Something to keep me partially occupied. But then, after finals, a couple of weeks to dwell on an empty house before summer school starts."

"We can call on the phone."

"We're students. I can't afford it. I barely survive now."

"So it's hopeless, you're saying."

"Feels that way. I don't want to think about it. Am I

going to see you again?"

"Nathan, live on that hope. Of course you will see me again. Don't you trust what we have? What we've been through together? About each other? All my explanations? We are going to see each other again and everything that implies. I have this summer in Freiburg for classes. Then next term. I will graduate at the end of the year, and shortly after that I will be in Africa somewhere. All this will occupy me, the pressure of school and the dream of going to Africa. But also wanting to see you again. Half a year from now I will be in Africa. I will be excited, and I will be sharing it with you in letters. I can't see past that, but I can see that far. The goodbye is a distraction for now, but we have a path."

I nodded approval at the promise of seeing her again in Africa. Somehow, this would lead to more plans. Hoping beat moping.

But then it was here. Her last day in Texas.

I almost didn't want to make love our last night together. It was more a sentimental moment than a bonding renewal.

"You seem glad to be going home," I said the next day as we walked to the car.

"Don't take it wrong, Nathan. I have loved so much our time together. But yes. I miss my home. I miss Germany and my studies in Freiburg. Now to see old friends. And I have so much to share with them. About you mostly. But everything that happened here."

"I know," I moaned. "God, I'm such a baby."

"I love you being a baby about this. But we've been apart before. And always the renewal was better. You will be okay."

I let out an exaggerated sigh for dramatic affect.

I couldn't think of anything to say on the way to the airport. Every time I tried to speak, it seemed stupid. Casual talk was all we managed.

"I'll see you soon," she assured me at the departure gate. "That keeps me going. I will see you soon. This isn't goodbye. It's 'until then.' And speaking of *Tomorrow Belongs To Me*.' Ha. Remember that scene in Cabaret? Just before that Nazi kid started singing the song that so enraptured us? The two main male characters in the movie, the rich playboy and the hero of the story, if you remember, they were having cocktails at the restaurant. And they toasted, 'to Africa.' Yes, Nathan. That's us. To Africa, my dear."

I was home before dark. The last thing I wanted to see was stars in the sky, so that was a plus. Once home, I could not concentrate on my studies, however. I gave up trying at midnight. An empty bed awaited me. I turned on the radio to distract my loneliness. And there it was. Don McLean singing the song "Vincent" with the opening line of "Starry Starry Night." Love was merciless. But I listened. It was of her. I knew I would see her again.

Chapter 34

I love Africa, Michaela's letter began. *It fulfills my wildest dreams to be here. I am in Zimbabwe. This is a country in southern Africa that was ruled by the British. They called it Rhodesia after the mining empire giant Cecil Rhodes. Such imperialism, I must say. But they speak English, and I am grateful. I remember how we used to talk, Nathan. All our dreams. And here I am living mine. Except without you. I missed you in Germany, but I knew I was coming soon to Africa and it kept me distracted. I am still distracted by my excitement to be here, but I do miss you. I feel it. But you will soon join me, I hope. You are almost finished with your studies. Make time to come here before you find your place in the professional world. I must share this marvelous experience with you. Or it will be diminished to me. So hurry, My Love. We enter a new phase now. New adventures too. Please find a way to come to Zimbabwe. I will be here for a year. Then I am not sure what I will do. I live in the capital city called Harare. Keep missing me.*

Your lover forever, Michaela

I could hear her voice and picture her excitement as I read the letter. I wasn't over missing her, but I had come to grips that this new phase was in order. She didn't stay stagnant in her life, and I wasn't going to in mine.

Africa. Zimbabwe, Africa. That had a ring to it. I

was going to go.

I did not look for even one job before, when I finished my bachelor's degree. And now that I was finishing my master's, a job was the farthest thing from my mind. As irresponsible as that was about me, I was confident I knew what I was doing. I was following some map inside of me that knew where it was going. I just didn't know how I was going to get there, which, as always, was part of the adventure.

Being a good student while in college gave me confidence. Someday I would have everything I wanted in life, including Michaela.

During my master's studies, I remained in the same house Michaela and I had shared. Her presence was always there for me, her memory always with me. The time flew by. Instead of job interviews, I looked at maps and read on southern Africa. This was the part of the continent the British explorer and missionary David Livingstone settled. That made things feel more familiar to me.

I had no money. I had student debt. Now I would have even more debt, but I was going to Africa. I pictured getting a job in the gold mines near Zimbabwe in South Africa. I had no idea if such a thing was possible. They had lucrative farms in Zimbabwe, I read, about the best in all of Africa. Maybe that would open something for me, some way to stay with Michaela.

Me in Zimbabwe. The thought boggled my mind. Me in Zimbabwe with Michaela. That seemed made in Heaven.

The flight to South Africa and on to Zimbabwe was horrible. I was stuck for seven hours in Zambia. Welcome to Africa, I was sure. If I had known of such a layover, I would have stopped in Lusaka and taken a bus the rest of the way to Harare. But a bus ride in this part of the world could have been seven days, for all I knew.

It was marvelous to look at Africa as I watched from the airplane window. So much vegetation. I did not see very much farmland, however. Mostly raw vegetation. Jungles, I assumed. What part of Africa was Tarzan from, I wondered?

Nervously, I looked for Michaela as I walked past the luggage belt. As usual, I did not check in my one lonely backpack that had accompanied me around the world. The luggage area was simply an indication that I was heading out of the airport.

"Nathan," I heard from nearby.

I looked and there she was, more beautiful than totally ever.

"Oh, Nathan, you came," she exuded as she ran to me. "You made it! I knew you would, but there is always that apprehension. Oh, Nathan. You must live here. But how? How long is your visa? Six months didn't you tell me in a letter?"

"Yes, six months," I concurred.

"Can you look for work? Are you allowed to look for work on this visa?"

"It's just a tourist visa. I'm American, so I'm supposed to be rich. They asked me how much money I had. I counted what was left of my student loan as tourist money for here. But I have a credit card now. I'll survive somehow. I can put off paying the loan for a while. I doubt I can work legally."

"You better not try black labor. They are so strict here. You will have to live on me. I am living on nothing, but things are cheap here. I have a place to stay, and food is cheap, so we will survive even on my small salary. It's so good to have you here, Nathan. There is so much to show you."

"I want to see Victoria Falls. And the Zimbabwe ruins. And I want to shoot the rapids on the Zambezi. God, I am in Africa. I can't believe it! This outdoes everything we've ever done."

"So many encores we've made, Nathan. It keeps getting better. I have six more months with my job teaching English. Just stay with me, and we'll see these places somehow. It is a large country, but not like Texas or Germany."

"Are there still white settlers here from the Rhodesia days?"

"Not so many now," she replied. "And you better watch what you say about Rhodesia and white settlers and such. There are tribal differences among the blacks here, but some real grudges against the white rule that just finished. Just be careful. Don't talk politics at all."

I put my arm around her while she led me to her car. With her small salary she still managed a car, an older version of the small Austin Mini she had in Freiburg.

I felt at home immediately. With all the familiarity we'd shared in Israel and Europe, in Texas and in Mexico, this was just another verse to our song.

Chapter 35

I had to find things to do while Michaela taught at her school. I loved to read and work out, so that filled some of the time. Being so limited in money kept me from going out very often. Even to look around.

I became bored and restless. Sometimes as I walked around Harare I came upon white Rhodesians/ Zimbabwe citizens.

"How are things for you?" I inquired of a man as I walked the streets of Harare.

"You mean me, a white that is now living with black rule?" he asked.

"Yeah," I replied with a nod.

"We're hopeful. The fears we have are based on being such a small minority of the population. We didn't allow the black vote before, from those fears. We'll see how it works. Right now, everyone is trying hard, but there are fears. Whites still have their farms. This is important, not just for the white farm owners, but Zimbabwe is self-sufficient in food because of it. We live day to day. We knew this reckoning would come, but we're hopeful. It is wrong to deny a segment of people the vote for any reason, but the fears we had—and still have—are the reason that happened. Rhodesia was prosperous for Africa and still is now as Zimbabwe. We can only pray it lasts. Many of the black tribes don't like one another, and each wants to dominate. We'll see what happens."

Later that night I told Michaela about my conversation with the white settler.

"I told you not to talk politics, Nathan. I knew you couldn't resist. It is dangerous. Not just because the government objects, but because we don't want to cause distrust or anger. I ask questions too, and talk, but I have been here longer than you. I have a sense who to talk to or how far I can go. I avoid it anyway. I love it here and love my job. We will be gone in a few months. I want you here. I love that you came. You are in a situation that is uncomfortable. Little money. Living off me. A foreign country that can be hostile to whites sometimes because of colonial memories. Most people want you here. Even blacks. They want to be a part of the big world, and they need tourism. Tourists with money is better, ha, but people want to get along. But you must not ask questions. Ask me and I'll try to answer."

"I understand, Michaela. I've been to a lot of foreign countries, as you know, some politically volatile and some hostile to Americans. I'll behave myself, but sometimes hearing from the horse's mouth, as they say, is interesting. Primary data, as we say in research."

"Okay, Nathan, but you have to be so careful."

"I know. But look, Michaela."

I handed her a small pamphlet I had found at a political booth. She read over it quickly.

"This is typical of what is happening now," she replied. "*Unfair competition,*" she read aloud from the pamphlet. She looked up at me, shaking her head in disgust. "There is a lot of sentiment among certain groups for communism. Not even socialism, as we think of it in Europe, but outright totalitarian communism. The right to take away any wealth and divide it. Go to work, pick up fair pay, live cheaply but securely. It sounds wonderful to many. But even many blacks here prospered under white rule during Rhodesia. I don't know what will happen next. But I love it here, and we will be gone in a few months. Notice things, but be careful. Be here with me. Keep loving me."

"It's good you remind me of the dangers of being white and asking political questions. I know this, but keep reminding me. I want to enjoy my time with you in your environment. So. I'll behave myself."

"What should we see this weekend, Nathan? On to better and safer topics. I get paid tomorrow. Let's splurge a bit. You've been stuck in the house. It's good to see a bit of Harare, but let's get out into the countryside now that I'll have some money."

"How far is it to Victoria Falls?" I asked her. "I've always wanted to see Victoria Falls."

"Several hours. Yes, it is wonderful. The largest waterfall in the world, right here where we live. Yes. Let's even spend the night in a hotel there. Really live it up. Eat in a nice restaurant. A Zimbabwe honeymoon."

I looked at her.

"Honeymoon, Michaela. That's a nice word."

"Maybe this is our last test. You in my world and living off me. And all we've already been through together. If we pass this test, if that is the word to use, maybe let's talk about marriage. I always wanted this with you, but we weren't ready. I think it is time."

I felt the tears welling up inside. I loved her honesty. I was glad we were coming to terms with marriage. But the realization overwhelmed me.

"Maybe we could get married here," I said.

"Wouldn't that be romantic?"

"The legalities are so complicated, Nathan. I'm sure it could be arranged. But we are two foreign white people from two different countries. We need to go home to get married."

"We are really talking about this. Like we're really going to do it."

"I do believe you are ready to settle down, and I can feel how I am. There is no one else I want to share my life with than you. We both know that of each other. Yes, I am ready. If something doesn't change all of that before we leave, then yes, let's get married. I adore the thought of that."

"Okay, but there are no legalities to a honeymoon. We'll spend our honeymoon while we're here. Starting with Victoria Falls."

"*Bestimmt*," she said.

"I almost forgot that word. Yes, *bestimmt*. For damn sure."

"So, Nathan, I will arrange to take leave from my school. I work for a German organization that supplies engineers and teachers to many underdeveloped countries. Because of the recent prosperity of Rhodesia, Zimbabwe is one of the better-off countries in southern Africa. In most of Africa, in fact. But it still struggles, and much of Zimbabwe has severe problems."

"Do you answer to your German organization mostly, or to Zimbabwe bureaucracy?" I asked.

"This German group adheres as much as possible to German labor laws. I have much leave time coming to me because of this. I saved them for your arrival. It is almost a thousand kilometers to Victoria Falls from Harare. The highway system is not good in much of the country. If we leave immediately from when I get off work next week, then with my leave time, and throw in a weekend, we can spend a couple of days and nights at Victoria Falls. Harare is in the northern part of Zimbabwe and so is Victoria Falls. But we are not as lucky as it sounds. Because so many of the roads are bad, we will have to travel a bit south as we go west to Victoria Falls. Bulawayo is the second largest city in Zimbabwe, so the best highway in the country is from Harare to Bulawayo. A slight detour because Bulawayo is in the southern half of the country. The roads are paved all the way to it, however. We can make good time, but we will have to travel hard."

The excitement of traveling again with Michaela, this time in her exotic domain, excited me, and the time flew. Soon, we were on our way to Victoria Falls as if passing through a time warp, it seemed.

A lot of the country we traveled was semi-arid, but parts included jungle areas. Many of the towns were small. There wasn't much traffic on the two-laned highway. If we got stuck behind a truck, however, it slowed us down.

"Zimbabwe is a landlocked country," Michaela commented as she drove. "But it makes up for it with Victoria Falls. Victoria Falls is not the highest waterfall in the world and not the widest, but it holds the largest volume of water of any in the world. Perhaps God gave them this waterfall to compensate for no ocean. The trade worked out, at least as far as beauty."

"So," I said to Michaela as I read from her guidebook. "Tell me if you heard any of this."

"Very good, Nathan. You are also a good navigator. It has been me doing the reading and instructing as we go along. It is nice to know I can count on you."

"Okay, here goes."

I read to myself for a moment, looking for the parts I wanted to share.

"Because of the mist coming from this largest body of falling water in the world," I read as we drove, "from a distance it often looks like smoke. So some tribe said…"

"Hey, some tribe said?" she mocked with a bite. "Tell me the name of the tribe. This is our home for now. Give me some detail. What tribe?"

"Would you have heard of them?"

"I don't know. Probably not. But I am learning more about the history and the tribes. Anyway, hey, tell me the name of the tribe."

"Well," I said with a sigh, "I don't see a tribal name here, but it is of the Sotho language."

"Sotho," she replied. "Like the tiny country nearby called LeSotho. It is like a tribal homeland inside of South Africa. Okay, that is close enough explanation, I suppose. At least some depth somewhere in the subject. So what were you going to say?"

"Would you like to hear the tribal name for the falls?"

"Of course. What do you think?"

"*Mosi-oa-Tunya*. That means 'the smoke that thunders.' "

"Oh, that is so clever. I love that. All the mist is like smoke, while the falls make such a thundering noise. Quite poetic, don't you think?"

I chuckled as I nodded yes.

"There was also another name for the falls," I continued. "An older one. It doesn't say how old, so don't get on my ass."

"Oh, Nathan, you poor dear. I must be so mean to you. So what is the older name?"

"Two names, actually, and I guess they mean the same thing. Two names, but only one meaning is given here. There is *Seongo* as one name and *Chongwe* as another. They both mean the 'place of the rainbow.' "

I looked up at her. She was wearing the same smile as me.

Chapter 36

"I wanted to leave with you," Michaela said. "But your visa expires before I am finished with my work here. I will be finished with teaching, but I have things to prepare before I leave. I did not think of this when I told you to come see me. I thought we could leave together because it is the end of the school year. But I have things with my organization to deal with before I go back to Germany. You will have to leave without me next week. We did not see much of Zimbabwe together. Thank God we saw Victoria Falls. Fort Victoria and the Zimbabwe ruins were interesting too, but I wanted to go around to the little towns more than we did. To get a feeling of the traditional people. Not just the 'city slickers' here in Harare, as you call them."

"I loved all we did together. But it is you I came to see."

"That's what you are supposed to say, and I believe you. But it is such a beautiful country, and I wanted to share more of it than we did. We enjoyed Harare and day-to-day life. But there is more to Zimbabwe than this and our few hotspots. I would love to live here."

"I would love to live here too, Michaela. We talked about it. We even flirted with thoughts about being Rhodesians if we had lived here in the old days. But the politics are unpredictable now. It could go any direction. I don't know if we would have a future here."

"Maybe it is good you must leave before me," Michaela commented. "Look for a job for us then. Find a place for us. Somewhere for me to join you. We'll get married as soon as we can. Now I think more good will come out of you leaving ahead of me than bad. Find out what I have to do to be a teacher in Texas or wherever it is you go."

"You will have to take a Texas history course to teach in a Texas school. Unless you get a job in a private school. Maybe there too. I just know Texas history is required to get a teaching certificate. My mother is a teacher and told me that."

"Why did you ask her such a thing?"

"We know we're going to get married. Germany, Texas, or wherever in America. So I told my mother that and asked her about you teaching. Just to get an idea."

"Okay, a sign from God, then, Nathan. All the more reason to go back to America and find your way. Wherever you choose, I will join you. But it sounds like Texas is where to look first. Probably I will be allowed to join you on a fiancée visa."

"But I can't stand anymore sentimental songs on the radio that stab at me wanting you there with me. Or watching the moon peer over the ocean torturing me about you."

"Or waterfalls, or starry, starry nights."

"Exactly. No. Not exactly. Better than exactly. *Bestimmt.*"

"Yes, *bestimmt*. But Nathan, this is the last time we are apart. We know what we want now. We seek it with a map from God. Getting our life set up will make the time pass. It will bring joy, not stabbings of loneliness. We are working for our future. We know we are ready.

And we've already spent our honeymoon. Now comes our life together as an official and bonded team. With children as interest on our loan."

"Is there any place you prefer to live in Texas, while I'm looking around? A place I should start?"

"I have no such notion, even with my stay with you in College Station. I don't know enough about life there to make such an idea of where I want to live. I wouldn't mind College Station, if you could get a job with the university there somehow. But I am sure I would love many places in Texas."

"Well, I already know I don't want to live in Houston. Or any other big city. Maybe San Antonio, even though it's a big city. You liked Galveston. It's on the beach."

"Yes, I loved Galveston. Try there first, if you like. Except there are hurricanes sometimes in Galveston. I do not know enough to suggest what I would like. Take care of me. Your baby. Your *Schatz*."

"*Meine Schatz*. Okay."

"I will be there in two weeks. I am certain you will not be ready for us to settle by then. So be on your way and know this was all planned by fate."

Chapter 37

The excitement soared as I watched Michaela walk into the baggage claim area at the Houston Intercontinental Airport. This marked the beginning—the beginning of not being separated ever again. I watched her movements as she looked around in anticipation of finding me. A huge smile broke onto her face when she spotted me. She seemed ready to run to me, then restored calmness and steadied her walk.

"We are really doing this," she said as we hugged. "We are really going to settle down."

"It gets even better," I replied. "A day after I called you in Germany, I found a job. We won't have to live on love. Or starve to death either."

"You found a job? My goodness. Where?"

"It's in Galveston. I have a master's in economics, but also know a little COBOL, the computer language. I talked to a couple of professors I'm in good stead with at A&M. Just for advice. One of these profs knew someone at Texas A&M-Galveston. It's called networking, you know. Another reason you go to a big, rich school. People know people. I gave a call to the high-tech department in admissions. A&M-Galveston is a true branch of Texas A&M. It got established as A&M's nautical branch. A&M is landlocked but got the jump on becoming not only a land grant university but a sea grant one, too. I know you don't know what I'm talking about, but we do research in things like engineering and agriculture. Ocean science as well. So A&M needed a port and started a branch for themselves a hundred miles away on the ocean. In Galveston. I got the job after my interview. They are getting more and more of their admissions computerized and needed someone immediately. I needed a job immediately. There you go. They bit."

"We have a job. I can't believe it."

"We'll register to get married there in Galveston. You'll need your visa and passport."

"I have my birth certificate also."

"We can be married in a month. I got us a studio apartment near our campus. You can look around with me to find something we like later on. Cheap. Has to be cheap. I not only have little money, but nothing saved up since I was a bum and a student so long. I have debts I have to pay off still."

"I have some money saved up," she offered.

"Keep it. You'll need it. I lived off you in Harare, you can live off me now."

"I'm just so excited to be here, Nathan. Once I decided to settle down, all my emotions fell into place. Since we are so poor, that means a small, simple wedding. I'm glad. That's all I want. I have no friends here. Your parents can be the witnesses. If you have a few friends that you feel you should invite, that is fine. But I want a small, cozy wedding. And moving into our new home or apartment will be our honeymoon. We're always on our honeymoon anyway. But Nathan, don't take off from work except the day we get married itself."

"Yeah. Sounds perfect, Michaela. All my best friends live far from here. My parents are enough to attend. In the meantime, Galveston is wonderful. We'll walk on the beach every day when I get home. The San Jacinto battleground is not too far away. That's where Texas won its independence from Mexico. There's a big monument to commemorate the victory. We'll visit it whenever we get out to unwind. And there is a wonderful restaurant there at San Jacinto. The battleship Texas is docked in the harbor there, too. We'll take my parents there when they come to the wedding. The restaurant will give us an excuse to visit the battleground every so often. And you haven't seen the Alamo yet, either. That's in San Antonio, a three-hour drive. That's plenty of excitement for us to break the monotony of getting established in our new lives."

She caressed my neck and pulled me down to kiss again.

"Everything we did together until now was just foreplay," she said. "It's like we did all we did just for this moment."

"I remember what you told me when I took you to Galveston for Christmas when you first arrived as a student to stay with me at A&M."

"What is that, Nathan? Powerful, dramatic longings of love to you?"

" 'I'm happy,' " I replied to her. "Those simple words you spoke were the greatest endearments anyone ever gave me. Now I want to say them to you. I'm happy, Michaela. I'm so incredibly happy."

A word from the author...

Born in Harlingen, Texas on October 7, 1948, where I grew up and worked on a cotton farm, I graduated from Harlingen High School in 1966. I attended Texas A&M beginning in Summer 1966. In January 1970 I dropped out to enlist in the United States Marine Corps, where I served as an enlisted man, attaining the rank of Sergeant, with an honorable discharge after three years.

I worked as a computer programmer afterwards in Houston and as a civil servant for a US Air Force Base in Frankfurt, Germany. I traveled and worked in Europe for two years, which included flying to Israel in October 1973 to aid the Jewish State in the Yom Kippor War. I was also in Greece in the summer of 1974 when the war between Greece and Turkey erupted over Cyprus. I was stuck on the Greek island of Ios for part of that war until I managed to catch a boat to Athens just in time to watch the Greek military dictatorship fold. I returned to Texas A&M in the fall of 1976 to finish my bachelor's degree in Business Management. I returned to Europe afterwards and also Israel, where I lived for almost a year. I later taught English in Taiwan before returning home in 1980 to get a master's degree in Agricultural Economics, which I received in 1982.

I joined the US Peace Corps in 1984 and served for three years in the Philippines. In 1987 I began work for the Swiss government as a computer programmer until 1998. I have worked in the IT department of Texas A&M since 1998. I have three children and am presently divorced. I am Jewish.

Thank you for purchasing
this publication of The Wild Rose Press, Inc.

For questions or more information
contact us at
info@thewildrosepress.com.

The Wild Rose Press, Inc.